Deception Pass

Matthew Tait

Matthew Tait pulls no punches in this story that is as intimate as it is imaginative, and his writing is eloquent and evocative in its violence, like a silk-enveloped gauntlet. I haven't felt so drawn in by a horror novel in a long time.
– Cameron Trost, owner of Black Beacon Books

TABLE OF CONTENTS

ALSO BY MATTHEW TAIT

<u>Novels</u>
Dark Meridian
Olearia
Slander Hall
Davey Ribbon
Providence Place
Schizoid

<u>Non-Fiction</u>
Different Masks: A Decade In the Dark

<u>Collections</u>
Ghosts In A Desert World

Part One

Shadows

Matthew Tait

1

Once again, Nick Wheeler woke up dead.

Not in a literal sense.

Though for all intents and purposes, his physical self was deceased. Like a workshop mannequin, his torso lay completely inert; his arms and legs, the same.

A rigid and immovable spike through his center, only Nick's spine gave any evidence of somatic sensation: a ghost echo, like a phantom limb, of the life it once contained. With sizeable effort and all instinct, Nick attempted to move his head, if just a centimeter – tried to thwart his lips into some semblance of a monkey's leer.

Nothing.

No movement of his body.

There was only the motion of sweat trickling down a face riddled with panic, and the discordant hum of a heart in turmoil.

Here we go again, ladies and gentlemen. Sleep paralysis for the third time this week.

Deep in the throes of an episode, Nick felt astonished at his ability to try and fight what was essentially un-fightable. He could spend all night here in his bed (and often did), endeavoring to move a part of his body, any part. Yet, the resultant outcome was always the same.

He *would not* be able to move.

No matter the force exuded or will expended.

In the end, it all added up to naught.

Paralysis would have him until dawn.

And so would the fear.

***

Within the framework of his chest, Nick's heartbeat resonated with familiar pings, almost electrical in nature. From his left earlobe came a subtle sound – a dirge not unlike an unbalanced washing machine. The sound itself was lonesome, forlorn, something whispered on a bad dream frequency. Although his eyeballs remained wide open and alert, there was no moving them beyond

4

the pure drive of animal instinct.

Beside him lay Heidi, his sleeping wife. Yet, she was beyond his grasp and as unreachable as his own body.

She may as well be on the moon.

Most maddening of all – at least to Nick – was a thing seldom discussed on social-media pages pertaining to sleep paralysis: a complete inability to move his tongue; a total surrender of his voice box and vocabulary. And though the act of swallowing could be accomplished with a limited degree of success, Nick's tongue remained rooted in its cavity like a slug caught in the death-vice of a mousetrap. In the stillness created by this complete lack of movement, Nick could also hear the inner machinations of his flesh going through autonomous motions: the whine of blood sloshing around his skull; the acoustic gurgle of his throat going through another rhythmic swallow.

Then, as if on cue, Nick perceived darkness from the corners of the bedroom – a heightening of shadows coming together as one.

Shadows. The Shadow Men.

As synonymous with sleep-paralysis lore as the stillness of the body itself, Nick had been subjected to Shadow entities for as long as he could remember. Oftentimes, their threat was minimal, mere prowlers at the subconscious door; other times, they came equipped with a menagerie of terrors so profound they tamed any horrors Nick worked with in the waking world.

Especially when they came with their leader.

The creature who wore a collection of hats – everything from balaclavas to berets – was another entity germane not solely to Nick's world. Doing the rounds with others susceptible to the phenomena, the Hat Man was a dark wildcard who danced with a malign, often authoritarian purpose. And though his presence was not always guaranteed, Nick had ascertained enough about his plight to understand the creature was perpetually

(in the shadows)

in the background, so-to-speak.

Urging his minions forward.

And here they came … generic Shadow Men filched from the generational nightmares of man. Mammalian in form but composed of an immaterial substance so dark the void between the stars seemed domestic by comparison.

One from the left.

And one from the right.

From Nick's position on his back, the tops of their heads were soon visible, followed by shoulder blades and the peeking proboscis of a snout. Sampling the air as they approached, Nick ascertained these strange creatures were enjoying the moment, enjoying his fear; somehow taking sustenance from it in exchange for rendering his flesh futile. *What are they?* he wondered for what must have been the thousandth time during this never-ending nightly cavalcade. *Who are they, and what do they want?*

Delicately, the right Shadow hovered over his unmoving face, its own head trained in a knowing manner: sardonic and mirthless. This close, its oval eyes became more than a sum of outlines, and Nick saw they embodied the white snow of dead-air television. The left entity, perhaps sensing Nick's utter unease during their last encounter, hovered somewhere just above his crotch.

God – Jesus, Nick thought in his ecstasy of terror. *If you're out there, please help me.*

An avowed atheist, Nick's litany to God could always be counted on when things were bad.

And things were definitely bad.

Closer now, the Shadow floated, its eyes oscillating between magenta and the readout of a television between channels. Bereft a mouth beyond a slit, Nick could nonetheless make out the syllables it was trying to form, a simple cadence both pitiless and bullying.

You're going to die, it gibbered, now suspended directly above Nick's head. *You're going to die. You're going to die. You're going to die.*

Possessing no capacity to scream, Nick's terror was nevertheless absolute. Inside, he raged and fought, trying (as he had on so many other nights) to send a signal to his sleeping wife – to somehow rouse her from her own torpor, so she could save him from these interlopers.

You're going to die. You're going to –

Below Nick's abdomen, pain exploded. White hot, three prongs attacked his genitals at once – like an arcade claw – gouging his testicles and attempting to lift them away as a prize.

Only recently discovering pain in their presence, the physical act receded in the face of the *incursion*, violating a part of Nick's body that should have been off-limits. Surely, demons, being things of the mind, were not permitted to wreak their havoc upon a person's physique.

Surely, they could look but never touch.

And whoever said they were demons?

At this juncture, what they were or were not seemed of little consequence. There was only this agony, even more potent because he could not attend to it. How long before this kind of assault made him bleed? How long before he suffocated under their taloned hands?

With the thought, something within Nick shifted subtly; a sliver of power returned to his eyes. Abruptly able to look down, he saw the gibbering

Shadow entity shrunken to the size of a midget, perched on his stomach like a gargoyle. On its features, something approaching a beatific smile, the slit it wore for a mouth uptilted in a way to suggest it was feeding on something.

Darkness clipped the edges of Nick's vision, this of a different order, the type heralding unconsciousness or sleep. Whichever, it was a blessed respite, a type of rescuing from creatures who, with each revolution of the night, inched closer and closer to snatching away his life.

2

Reaching up on tiptoes to manhandle a plate from a cupboard, Heidi asked, 'How bad was it?'

Nick, ogling a breakfast of raisin toast with morning eyes, did not reply. Hayley Wheeler, thirteen years old this coming March and sole child of Nick and Heidi, stared across the table at her father with a forlorn expression. Owl lenses magnified her eyes. Hayley had listened to similar exchanges between her parents for most of her adolescent life, and something about Nick's posture must have given her pause.

Nick licked his lips.

'Bad,' he managed at last.

His wife, having liberated the plate, came over

to the table. 'Then you shouldn't go into work today, should you? Andrea can finish the shoot.'

'I seem to recall having this conversation before,' Nick said. 'Many times. Andrea doesn't really know what she's doing. And if we want a commission –'

'I don't care about the commission,' Heidi said, speaking in the flat syllables birthed into her vocabulary since having Hayley. 'Look at yourself. Go look in the mirror. Look at your *eyes*.'

It's not my eyes that are the problem this time, Nick thought with his usual dollop of acerbity. *It's my crotch, Heidi. Feels like I've been attacked with a scythe down there.*

Recollections of being grappled with the three-pronged metal claw threatened to surge, but Nick stifled the memory.

'Nothing more coffee won't fix,' he said, managing something approximating a grin. 'Get me some, please?'

Beneath the table, Nick felt the soft kick of Hayley's moccasin, and he looked up to find her smiling in turn.

'Careful,' she said.

It was an old joke, but one carrying mainstay power when sharing a house with two girls. Occasionally, Nick would revert back to a 1950s curmudgeon, complete with the lexis of *Go make*

11

me a sammich, woman. The running joke was a special kind of relief … because outside these walls, parts of the country seemed to be sliding back into those dark ideological epochs of history.

'Can you at least make another appointment with Helen?' Heidi said while gravitating toward the coffee machine. Helen was Nick's general practitioner going on twelve years; one of the few people outside his family well-versed in the labyrinthine world of sleep paralysis. 'You know she'll probably see you without a proper appointment. She likes you, Nick.'

'Maybe a little *too* much,' he said, and winked at Hayley.

Another gentle kick with her moccasin.

He said, 'You know the drill. In a few hours, the episode will feel like a depraved memory. By tonight, a bad dream. Andrea said she'd meet me at the top of the Canlis building …' Nick consulted his phone. 'At ten. And I'm going to be there, complete with equipment. *You* may not care about the commission, but how else are we going to keep Hayley here in proper makeup?'

In riposte, Hayley poked her tongue out, running it over dense black lipstick. As a young girl straddling the fringes of a conceited Goth, giving *voice* to any complaint concerning her chosen lifestyle would probably be deemed superficial or lame.

'You joke now,' Heidi said, returning to the stove and igniting another burner. 'But I'm the one who has to sleep with you.'

Nick returned his gaze to the raisin toast, his appetite void. Being reminded of how much Heidi sacrificed by acquiescing to be his lover – a task she had been living with for close to fifteen years – was always a hard pill to swallow. There was his sleep paralysis, of course, but there was so much more: night terrors stemming directly from his occupation; having to wade every day through the kind of subject matter that made other people squirm. Sure, Heidi Wheeler *also* belonged to the Gothic brigade; a woman who could still head-bang to *Metallica* and *Alice In Chains* with the best of them. But …

But having an innocent predilection for the macabre during your twenties is worlds away from living with the real thing in your forties.

Any other woman (upon first learning the finer details of Nick's childhood trauma, for instance) might have bolted for the hills then and there. But Heidi Campbell, the resolute and stoner Goth chick who once moonlighted as an actress in low-budget horror films, had prevailed – eventually accepting Nick's offer to take on the name *Wheeler*. It was a marriage that would go on to eventually secure a lifelong association with a vast catalogue of terrors

… terrors that, in all probability, made those past low-budget features seem tame.

'Dad?' Hayley asked. 'Can you email me the results after you finish today? I swear on my life they won't go anywhere near Instagram this time.'

Nick pushed away from the table. Quickly, he stepped deftly over to his daughter, leaning in to kiss the top of her head. 'We'll see. I should be done before you get home from school – you can take a look then.'

Hayley appeared disappointed but resigned. He maneuvered over to his wife (now busy with a variety of dishes) and planted a soft one on the back of her neck. Though he couldn't see her face, Nick *felt* a wicked smile like an image through the lens of a camera. He could also feel her love … an inexpressible and raw sentiment between two people who seldom wandered from each other's sight.

'I'll make an appointment with Helen when I'm done. It's about time I tried a different tact, anyway.'

She turned around to face him, all smiles and fortitude. 'You promise?'

'I swear it on the River Styx.'

Then her arms were around him, one still gripping a washcloth, the other mired in bubbles. Despite Hayley's playful protestations, Heidi leaned in for her own kiss … this one deep, prolonged, and pungent with coffee.

'Do you mean it?' she asked when they finally detached. 'Back home before Hayley?'

'Just need that final money shot. Then we're done.'

Exiting the house, Nick discovered a bounce in his step he could not have foreseen after the horrors of the previous night. Heidi and Hayley, perhaps sensing on some visceral level the tragedy to come, even deigned to serenade him goodbye from the front porch, watching and waving as he sped off into the day.

Chased solely by the shadows of the morning, he thought.

3

A bloated and desiccated neck. Distended eyes. Purple rot-infused, gritty cheeks imbued with dead cells. Though the illusion of death was almost absolute, the model would occasionally blink, shattering the fantasy.

'Put out your tongue a little ways,' Nick said. 'So it's lolling.'

The model followed his instruction. With tongue protruding, Andrea skipped brazenly into the shot and applied a dollop of makeup. Retreating, her subtle smile relayed she was pleased with her handiwork.

Nick was pleased, too.

'Hold your breath,' he told the model. 'For at

least thirty seconds, if you can.'

She did so, and again Nick went to work, snapping multiple shots at shutter speed with his Canon EOS. First the bugging eyes and discolored face, then the whole body, swaying on both a real tether and an invisible one. The one not visible kept the girl afloat without injury. The visible one was a fashioned noose of thick rope fastened around the girl's jowls, her chosen method of suicide. Earlier, Andrea had hosed the front of her engorged labia with apple juice – the effect providing an illusion the wanton act had caused an involuntary voiding. Though such techniques barely registered on film, Nick prided himself on small attentions to detail.

Finally, the model opened her eyes, unable to hold her breath any longer.

'I need a cigarette,' she declared. 'Please take this thing off me for five goddamn minutes.'

Under his breath, Nick cursed. Time and again, the models he employed were given fair warning about the methods used for these projects; yet, time and again, they wanted to bail when things got heated.

He glanced over at his assistant.

Andrea stared back at him with a coy, somewhat shamefaced smile.

'No worries,' said Nick. 'We'll take five. But …'

'Cassandra,' the dead girl deadpanned.

'Sorry – Cassandra. Can you smoke out on the balcony, please? This whole place is like one giant tinder box.'

***

'Where did you find this one?' he asked Andrea when the girl had gone. 'Somewhere on Craigslist?'

'Oh, come on. She's not *that* bad. At least my makeup makes up for any shortcomings.'

Nick laughed. 'Makeup makes up?'

'I'm unconsciously hilarious.'

'Your skills with a brush have never come into question,' Nick said. 'I just wish you knew how to handle a camera.'

'That's where *your* skills come in, my dear.' Andrea brandished the phone cradled in her hand. 'I can't even take a decent selfie with this thing.'

'But you can navigate Twitter and hold a conversation, simultaneously. That has to count for something.'

'Touché.'

Reaching for his own device, Nick hesitated ... the surroundings instead claimed his attention. Today's office was the top floor of Seattle's Canlis building, a deserted fifth floor. Once this room had been a four-star dining experience; now it was unadulterated chaos, the superfluous flotsam and jetsam of a bustling restaurant trade. In addition to tables resting on their backs, dozens of chairs had been assembled in the epicenter, a prelude to a pyre. The mound's architects, having created a safe haven for potential vermin, had seemingly departed at the eleventh hour in lieu of lighting a match.

Doing so, they inadvertently created a suitable backdrop tailored for those who took pictures for a living.

Pictures of suicide; pictures of death.

And all of it a complete fabrication.

Fashioned through the tools of digital photography and practicality, with in-camera special effects.

'I can't,' Andrea said, as if reading his thoughts. 'I just can't fathom how people pay money for what you do. Who is your client this time?'

'This time? I can honestly say I don't know. And that's the way I like it. He or she could be a wealthy politician – or they could be some fourteen-year-old kid sitting behind a computer in their mother's basement.'

'And as long as they pay up, it simply doesn't matter to you?'

Though the room's destroyed windows gave

little illumination, Nick could still see his assistant's face etched out in stark relief: pixie features just falling short of true beauty; her trendy and sharp hair dyed a shade of purple in keeping with the identity of someone who dabbled in the arts. Not for the first time, Nick felt a tickle of irritation at the question ... for here was a woman who was *also* receiving payment for services rendered.

Just because you don't pull the trigger, my dear, doesn't make you any less culpable.

'Half upfront, half when the job is done. No, it doesn't, Andrea. This isn't the industry of snuff, and we're not hurting anybody.'

'You don't think –'

'That some of our clients carry out some of these fantasies? No, I honestly don't. Some of them probably beat-off to it, I have little doubt of that. But I don't think for a second, any individual has ever offed themselves from studying a bunch of images.'

Death, he thought. *Ever the great taboo.*

Nick could sense Andrea working up the courage to say more, but Cassandra chose that moment to return from her nicotine fix, a zombie in human form. Looking at her, it wasn't hard to rescind his previous meditation ...

Perhaps death wasn't some great taboo, after all.

Because here it strode around with all the casual finesse of the living.

Cassandra, with portions of her rib cage protruding as she walked, said, 'Let's get this fucking thing over with then. Tonight, I have to suck someone's dick, and I can't very well do it looking like this, can I?'

***

For his final shots, Nick ascended a collection of abandoned work platforms to obtain an aerial view of Cassandra's motionless body lying on the cement; her dress hiked up, and a pool of fake blood suppurating from a cracked head. Provisionally, these were 'aftermath' images to the girl's strangulation; the subject's bulk succumbing to gravity after the hangman's noose had frayed and failed. Although the client had not requested such an epilogue, Nick would often devise (while working) additional concepts to both his and Andrea's original ideas.

A lifeless plunge to a second death, he thought from his raised perch. *There's a weird kind of symmetry to it all.*

Balking at the idea, Andrea cautioned against the danger climbing such a hazardous and time-worn structure, pointing out if he made it to the top, there existed the possibility of falling, himself.

'I'm not going to the top,' he argued, staring intently at the apex and wondering how he would manage to do exactly that. 'That third tier underneath should be more than sufficient. Look, they're made out of steel. I reckon I'll be fine.'

'Oh, you *reckon*? Since when did this kind of risk-taking hinge on some dubious, half-assed assessment?'

Choosing not to reply, Nick shouldered his camera and began the ascent, making good on his word until the third tier. Then, with only a cursory glance at the two girls, proceeded to manhandle his way up to the fourth … followed by the fifth. Andrea, perhaps knowing her complaint wouldn't carry, beckoned Cassandra into position, arbitrarily decanting red corn syrup with a fat plastic syringe onto the concrete.

With Andrea finally out of the way, Nick's sole object through the viewfinder of his digital camera was a dead girl wearing a green dress.

He thought: *This is how snipers must feel, seeing the quarry laid low.*

Pressing the shutter release button, Nick's index finger instead slid on its face. Perspiration (both from the climb and occupying the enclosed box of a building) was making inroads over his wrists and hands, transforming the camera into a slick potato.

A few calming breaths ensued.

But Nick felt no better.

Just get the final shot and get out. Who cares if it isn't perfect.

Eyes through the viewfinder again, and suddenly it was Andrea he was looking at: Andrea with her guts ripped out while a business of flies supped from her eyes. Where her cheeks had been, metal spikes protruded, the open maw of her mouth now a shattered envelope of teeth and gums.

Nick reeled back and closed his eyes, hoping to scour the illusion. Opening them, he slowly brought one eye back to the single lens. Now it was only Cassandra down there, her puddle of blood having widened considerably. Before the vision could make a comeback, Nick quickly snapped a shot, then another, filling the camera with close-ups of veins gone to seed like the surface membrane of rotting fruit.

On his sixth picture, the Shadows appeared.

Seen through the screen, their dimensions were altered to dark smudges the size and width of his thumbprint.

Nick had little doubt these were the same entities from last night: Shadow monsters that walked and stalked Nicholas Wheeler's nocturnal life. Moments went by as he did nothing but observe them, as though watching villainous cartoons through the display of a cell phone.

It's not me they're interested in.

Today, the creatures had eyes solely for his actress, sniffing her out like vultures at the scene of carrion, inhaling her ejected life with the finesse of hummingbirds at a bower. Cassandra, perhaps on some deep level intuiting their proximity, lifted her head the barest of inches. The Shadows, seeing the evidence of deception at work, retreated as though scalded.

And turned their attentions upward.

Toward the man holding a camera.

In concert with their gaze, Nick's body suddenly froze, his anatomy yielding to a state where even the fine hairs broaching his wrists went static. His sight (still secured on the camera) was granted a view of his tormentors' faces: vulpine brows atop eyes more in league with a serpent's than the snow of static television. It was as if, granted access to daylight, the illusions of their Shadow selves were sloughing away.

With no ability to keep his balance, Nick felt his body teeter, slacken, and begin to slide. Loosened from his frozen grip, the camera fell first, somersaulting, yet still managing to capture the waiting Shadows each time the lens revolved.

It mattered little because Nick could see them

clearly: snouts upturned and orifices agape.

Nick's body finally curved over the platform's edge.

Falling, he heard shouting. Andrea was on the brink of panic, yet her din was peripheral, far away.

Below, the Shadows waited like patient bloodhounds.

Still unable to move, Nick fell into a long darkness.

And dreamed of another time.

Part Two

Secret School

1

Deception Pass in Seattle spreads over four thousand acres of land, rugged cliffs, and furtive coves hugging a dramatic seascape of swift current and whirlpools. Primarily known as a strait separating Whidbey Island from its sister, Fidalgo, with a two-lane manmade bridge conjoining them, many people living on the outskirts of Washington remain unaware of the state park's secret grottos and old-growth forests. Receiving its peak intake of humanity during the warmer seasons (where up to two million flock to the coast's premier hiking trails and campsites), winter can often serve as a popular alternative for the recluse-minded, those seeking a singular kind of solitude.

Like local family of six, the Wheelers.

It was during the mid-Eighties that Chad Wheeler (who had one more child after the addition of Nicholas in March of 1975) was offered an extended sabbatical from his teaching position at Seattle University. His wife, Wendy, the biological mother to only one of their four children, served as a chief architect; she decided they would maintain a small lodging in Deception Pass just north of Hoypus Point – a property built close to a minor slope overlooking the ocean.

Then aged twelve, Nicholas Wheeler – a middle school student known simply as *Nick* or *Ferris Wheel* to those in his immediate circle – stood on the cusp of a different kind of education in the ominous landscape of Whidbey Island.

***

With only three bedrooms, the cabin was full … though Nick was sometimes hesitant in referring to their place as a cabin. Crapbox, he'd once proclaimed it; the moniker applied when the central heating failed to properly live up to its namesake during the colder days and nights. Chad's brood of children, while typically well-behaved during summer and school, would often turn into monsters during Chad's sabbaticals in Deception Pass.

Wendy attributed their moods to a different, less stringent diet; Chad credited their rebelliousness to winter's tempest, a known contributor effecting seasonal serotonin levels.

'Seasonal serotonin levels?' Wendy asked him one night after tucking in Bianca, their youngest and her only child by Chad. 'You made that up.'

'No. It's true, I swear,' Chad replied, grinning broadly from his position on the couch. 'I read it in *Human Events* magazine.'

Wendy slumped down next to him. 'Oh, now I *do* believe it. Because all your bullshit comes from the conservative magazines. No – it's two things, really. The level of sugar you let them have … and their freedom to basically do whatever they please. Which gives them confidence to challenge our authority.'

'Louise is flirting with becoming a vegetarian, so you can't blame the sugar there. And Nick –'

'Needs a different type of discipline. There I said it.'

Chad let out a resigned sigh. This was one topic he often navigated delicately, like a skier through prickly terrain. His second wife, Wendy, had never been a fan of his youngest child.

'Nick is … strange,' Chad finally conceded. 'The boy wants to be some kind of artist. I've heard that all artists are a little loopy.'

Wendy's lips pursed, an expression bordering on a grimace. 'Loopy? The boy's twelve and still experiences night terrors like a child half his age.'

'Artists are *supposed* to have vivid imaginations. Or so some of the faculty say. As a man of numbers, I wouldn't know. Wendy, he was close to his mother. He hasn't been quite the same … or as *resilient* as Sebastian or Louise.'

Wendy's grimace expelled a huff. 'I don't foresee him becoming any kind of artist, Chad. On his current path, he'll wind up a drunk and will be mooching off you until the day you die. Why can't you see him for the way he really is instead of making excuses every time we have this discussion? Good Lord! If Bianca went around like he does – always with his nose in one of those silly books ...'

'Hey, I went through a space phase, remember?'

'And you grew out of it. The crazy thing is, Nicholas actually thinks it might have something to do with his night terrors. When reading all that junk is probably what's *causing* it.'

Chad was on the precipice of saying more. Much more. How Nick had consented to playing sports when school started back up again. How his grades (exempting athletics, of course) were more than satisfactory. But Chad knew, all too intimately, Wendy's bolshiness once she latched onto something. Like a tiger with a morsel, he once confided to a friend – her inability to let go until the bitter end.

'I'll talk to him,' Chad said, knowing he would be doing no such thing. This was simply a way to appease the tiger. 'Try to get him to spend more time with his brothers and sisters this season. Maybe Sebastian's new-found interest in girls will rub off some.'

***

Unknown to the adults, a shadow crouched in the doorway of the opposite bedroom, eavesdropping. Though Nick did not manage to catch the entire conversation, he heard enough. The *gist*, his friend Saul might have said.

Wendy hates me. And there isn't a damn thing I can do about it.

Nick's father did not hate him, but his attitude on many occasions – forever conceding to his wife's demands – often felt as equally distressing. During some of Wendy's more spiteful moments, he sometimes thought of Chad as a coward, completely under lock-and-key to someone who had entered their lives only three short years ago.

Tonight's conversation, while overall containing nothing Nick hadn't heard before in some capacity, had still been peppered with enough red flags to warrant the first seeds of an escape strategy.

Every kid dreams of running away somewhere – and every kid reaches the same stumbling block: Where on earth will I go?

Before it could creak, Nick gently latched his door shut and stepped back into the safe shadows of his bedroom. Through the gloom, Sebastian's snores could be heard; his brother dreaming of motor cars, baseball, and making Chad proud. The siblings (while possessing a conventional aptitude to love one another) were too different to ever warrant becoming friends. Or so Sebastian liked to assert, often while holding his younger brother down and punching his arms repeatedly.

You're a freak, Ferris Wheel. That's why Dad chose to give you the middle name Ferris – because you remind everyone of a Ferris wheel. That is, you're completely loopy and a source of amusement.

Nicholas *Ferris* Wheeler.

What strange compulsion had compelled his mother and father to arrive at that one?

Stepping over to his bed, Nick shuddered at the thought of lying down. Though sleep had been a thing both welcomed and embraced throughout elementary school –

Nick was even a staunch fan of afternoon naps after Saturday T-ball – everything forever changed after his tenth birthday.

As if this double-digit threshold sent warning signals to outside parties.

Outside parties who had the power to control his body and render it frozen.

Since then, Nick often dreaded sleep, sure in the knowledge Shadow creatures would pay him a visit.

And a Shadow wearing a hat would be leading the charge …

Nightmares, his father concluded – and the doctors had initially agreed. Nothing more than hallucinations brought about by the death of his biological mother, her departure during a pivotal time when he needed her most. Psychologists, unable to control the elusive threat with basic medication, insisted Nicholas undergo a few weeks of supervised sleep in a clinical environment. Nick, having arrived at complete despair from periods of episodic insomnia, acquiesced to this course of action.

Much to the surprise of his family.

But then Wendy Fuller abruptly entered their lives.

And specialists – in addition to tackling his nightmares with medications and sleep studies –

were just as swiftly off the table.

Growing boys, Wendy reasoned, simply needed a special brand of tough love if they were to sleep soundly at night.

<u>2</u>

The next morning, Nick was relieved to report his sleep was free of boogeymen. Though this wasn't something he recounted. His father, over a breakfast table of porridge, would make secret eyes. If Nick chose to return the look, this was an unspoken *all clear* signal the night had been without incident. Today, the first day of December, every kid in the Wheeler clique had decided to pull up a chair.

And Nick had an inkling why.

'Dad?' Sebastian inquired. The boy was on his third piece of toast, lips plastered with strawberry jam. 'Is it okay if Louise, Bianca, and I go on a ride today? On the four-wheelers. I want to teach Bianca how to ride properly.'

Wendy was happy to chime in whenever her daughter's name was mentioned. 'She already knows. We used the Hayfield's paddock last year for one glorious afternoon. Didn't we, sweets?'

Her brown eyes wreathed by prescription glasses more akin to goggles, Bianca ignored her mother. This morning her attentions were reserved solely for the small, portable television broadcasting cartoons from the counter.

'Yeah, but that was piggy-backing with you,' Sebastian said. 'You were essentially doing all the legwork. Today, I'll teach her how to do it solo. I'm old enough, aren't I?'

'Whether a fifteen-year-old boy is old enough is not the issue,' said Louise, happy to play the bookish contrarian. 'It's your skills. And you, Sebastian, ride that thing like a lout.'

'It's called confidence,' Sebastian re-joined. 'I crank it some because I know what I'm *doing*. Ferris Wheel, can you please pass me the butter?'

Though Sebastian was all smiles and batting lashes, Nick felt the subtle prong of his brother's sneaker jabbing his shin. *Hurry up*, the jab said. *My request is a demand and not an invitation*.

Obliging, Nick slid the margarine tub over, pushing it with the tip of a knife.

Wendy condemned Nick's chosen method with

a disapproving stare.

Without looking up from his paper, Chad said, 'How about on one condition? How about you let Nicholas tag along with you today? Nick would like a four-wheeling lesson, wouldn't you, Nick? The four Wheeler kids riding a four-wheeler.'

Breaking her self-exiled silence, Bianca cackled.

Before Nick could reply, Louise said, 'No, Nick *doesn't* want to go riding the four-wheeler today, do you, Nick? That's because our little Ferris Wheel here has found himself a new friend.'

All eyes zeroed in on him, their collective scrutiny like physical heat. Before he could deflect the question, it was Sebastian who broke the moment again, testifying that *imaginary* friends did not constitute the real thing.

'Is it that lovely Rosa from down the street?' Wendy asked, her voice betraying she wasn't all that keen on the notion.

'No, it's a he,' Louise went on. 'Only *he's* an old man, some kind of weirdo. Hangs around on those bluffs near Mount Erie all day. Doing what? I don't know. Just stands there mooning at the sky.'

'He's not a weirdo,' Nick said quietly.

Eyes bore down on him again, hot with questions. Why was Nick talking to some old man? Why was he hiking the slopes close to Mount Erie?

Some of those were *dangerous*. Any explanation Nick offered wasn't going to fly, so he asked (rather politely) to please be excused ... old-fashioned etiquette only coming into being with Wendy's arrival.

'No, you may *not* leave the table,' his father said. Having abandoned his paper, Chad Wheeler was now hunched forward over the table, nose pinched, on the precipice of a performance for one: his wife. 'Tell me more about this man. What's his name? And why haven't you mentioned him before?'

Nick shot his sister a look. 'I *did* mention him. In confidence.'

In return, Louise made a face.

'Well, I don't want you going up there again. Not today or any other day. Today, you'll join Sebastian, Louise, and Bianca.'

Still in his quiet voice, Nick said, 'I will *not*.'

Chad's eyes grew, then grew some more. Receiving backtalk was one thing; receiving it close to the woman who forbade it was simply *untenable*. Before his father could rise, Nick pushed his seat away from the table, his breakfast now cold.

'When are *you* going to be the one talking, Dad. Instead ...' Nick waved a hand in Wendy's direction without looking at her. 'Instead it's *her* always doing the talking. You're like one of those zombie ants they told us about at school. Do you know what happens to them? A fungus takes over their brain, and they turn into zombies. And that's what you are … a mouthpiece for something else.'

Silence greeted this revelation. Engaged in the act of mastication, all three siblings ceased chewing. Faintly, Nick could hear the sound of Bugs Bunny provoking Elmer Fudd, his underhanded method of torture this time was an act of cross-dressing. *I've gone too far*, he thought, wondering if he should apologize to break the tension. *Really put my foot in it.*

On the verge of doing just that, some wilder part of his nature took pleasure in his family's slack-jawed incredulity. They thought him meek, those faces, and often took delight in his submissiveness. Well, no more. Fear at night was one thing, but having it take center stage during the day was something Nick would no longer tolerate.

Without bothering to speak, he turned around and pushed through the kitchen entrance, then through the living room, and finally out the backdoor.

Greeted by a day already threatening the first inches of snow.

***

Though multiple paths led away from the cabin, Nick only ever used one. A furtive route that had, by degrees, come to feel personal. Beginning in a depression between a riot of sarsen, this trail meandered into a large wood of Douglas firs. Often tempted to share his find, Nick remained resolute in keeping the mystery tight-lipped.

More than foul upon his dramatic exit from the house, Nick's mood soon brightened. The path (presently covered with alkaline layers of morning frost) was still clear enough to properly navigate. On either side of its borders, the Douglas firs swayed to a sea-scented breeze, now minimal, compared to the gale of the previous day.

This is where I belong, thought Nick, and there was no part of him that disagreed with the sentiment. Deception Pass, though isolated from arcade games and movie theaters, still held enough casual enchantment far removed from night terrors or bullying brothers. Trudging the path, Nick intercepted chipmunks, squirrels … and even the occasional fox. Their inner lives, like microcosms of rationality compared to his own dysfunction, seemed to serve a part of his being that Nick presently had no vocabulary for.

Saul would tell you it's probably the spiritual part, he thought, spying the path's end through the current copse of trees. Where the Douglas firs ceased, a steep embankment of frosted grass began. *He would say their black eyes are a reflection of the eternal ...*

Nick smiled, pleased with the analogy. Though Saul Kidman entered his life only a short time ago, the old man's words were beginning to feel like a proper education. Certainly, more suitable than anything taught at Cherry Crest Elementary; a place where the teachers regarded him with the same level of hostility his peers did.

It's because they're intimidated by you, Saul confided one day. *They see something in your eyes that frightens them.*

Whether this was true mattered little, because for the first time an adult was talking to him as a friend ... if not an outright equal. Nick's self-esteem, having taken a daily battering from a tribe who considered him a freak, was now being lifted. And it was an alien sensation, this concept of self-respect. His stepmother, Wendy, having extolled in Nick the art of self-hatred, simply didn't know what to do with his newfound confidence.

And I owe it all to a crazy codger who spends his days watching the sky for angels and UFOs.

***

He was sweating by the time he reached the

summit, sure in the knowledge Saul wouldn't be in his usual spot; that perhaps today, Nick had made the ascent for nothing.

'Boy!' Saul shouted. He was seated in a cheap, portable chair only feet from the slope's edge. 'I thought you might not be coming today. Told myself our sighting might have scared you off for good.'

Nick, still huffing from the climb, smiled as he approached. 'Mr. Kidman – that was an *airplane*.'

'No anti-collision lights that I could see. No landing lights, either. It *did* look like it came out of Ault Field, though. Didn't it? Might be my glasses weren't fixed on properly.'

On the slope's flat portion, the blue waters of Deception Pass became visible: the small white-capped waves; the glistering horizon. And all of it was like being inside a framed portrait of striking coastline. Though Nick frequented this particular slope many times, the sight of all that blue never got stale. Reaching Saul, he said, 'You brought hotdogs? What will we cook them with?'

The old man regarded him with something like mischief, his lips partially visible through a mat of coarse facial hair not quite a beard. 'As long as we don't make a habit of eating them raw, I won't tell if you don't.'

Saul's mention of secrecy prompted Nick's

next words.

'I've done something stupid,' he said. '*Really* stupid. I might have accidentally told my sister about you.'

No surprise registered on the old man's face; only indifference.

'She was bullying me as usual. Going on about having no friends. That sort of thing. She's such a cretin when she wants to be. She –'

'It doesn't matter,' Saul told him, waving away the declaration. 'You and I, we've nothing to hide. *Look,* Nick. Over there.'

Nick looked, following the tip of Saul's pointing finger to a bulky array of incoming clouds.

'Mammatus?' he ventured. 'Or maybe Anvil?'

'Neither. Though I'm not interested in the clouds. Look what's on *top* of the clouds.'

On the cusp of rejecting Saul's find (they could play this game more than once a day), something bright snagged Nick's vision near the top of the grouping clouds. By degrees, this brightness shifted into a rectangle: green on the outside; spheres of pink in the middle.

Nick said, 'It looks like a cigar.'

Donned in his winter best (a black trench coat as ancient as himself), Saul fumbled around in its pockets, never once taking his eyes off the apparition in the sky. Soon his clumsy search yielded a Polaroid camera, recently bought and paid for in one of the park's tourist kiosks.

'See the way it shifts?' said Saul, his voice partially muffled as he began to take pictures. 'Almost like it's transparent? Some great minds posit things like this might actually be alive, and we can see through them like jellyfish swimming through the water. Here, take a look.'

In his rush to grab the camera, Nick almost fumbled the thing. Then it was in his hands and up to his eyes. Years later he would determine *this* very moment – raising Saul's Polaroid camera to his right eye – was the beginning of a love affair with the heft and weight of something that could immortalize moments of time.

'I see it!' he shouted. And he could, too. The pinkish parts of the object had grown somewhat, spheroid shapes jittering like life under a microscope. 'What do you think it is, Saul? What *could* it be?'

Saul's hands were full again, this time with a pair of binoculars. 'If I knew the answer to that one, I wouldn't be up here every day. Whatever it is, it's *unidentified*. So that makes it a UFO. Wouldn't you agree?'

'I guess so. Oh, I think it's gone. No wait … yes. It's gone. I can't see it anymore.'

Saul put down the binoculars, a drawn-out sigh

escaping his belly. Then he picked up the polaroid pictures and began waving them about. 'It's vanished; it hasn't even hit nine in the morning, and we're down for a sighting already. These are good odds for the rest of the day. Say, Nick, have you given any thought to what we talked about yesterday?'

His attention still riveted on the now empty patch of sky; it took Nick a few seconds to comprehend the query. Their last exchange, he remembered, concerned his night terrors and hallucinations. For some mystifying reason (even to himself), Nick had disclosed just about everything.

Maybe because Saul is the only person who'll believe me ...

'I have,' Nick replied. 'And I read the article you gave me. Is it true there are hundreds of people all over the world who experience the same thing I do?'

'Hundreds we *know* about,' said Saul. 'Most people who encounter the phenomena are often too scared to talk about it – even to loved ones. They're afraid of not being taken seriously.'

Nick thought about Wendy's expression when he'd confessed that sometimes he awoke at night physically paralyzed. Her look hadn't reflected disbelief ... but something approximating disgust.

'I can understand why. And you think some of

these things I see might actually be *real*?'

'I wouldn't discount the possibility. After all, there are more things –'

'In heaven and earth than are dreamt of in the old philosophies,' Nick finished, and grinned.

'That's right.'

Turning around to face Nick properly, his gray eyes occluded by rose-tinted glasses, Saul studied his young protégé with some satisfaction. 'You catch on quick, young Nick. The truth is, I don't really know what's happening to you. If what you experience at night has … supernatural properties or not. Give me some time, though, and I'll find out. If you'd like, we can find out together.'

***

On their first encounter, Nick was more than apprehensive, ready at a moment's notice to bolt away from the stranger should he exhibit even the most timid threat. Although his older sister *was* a cretin, Louise was definitely right about one thing: weirdoes were everywhere in America. And you only had to turn on a television at six o'clock to discover this.

But Saul allayed his fears soon enough, cracking jokes about the weather and what it was like to be an old man with arthritis. When Nick asked the question as to *why* an old man with arthritis was braving a cold slope (surely it wasn't for the view alone), Saul reached into an oversized duffle bag by a collapsible chair and produced a tattered magazine. Looking down, Nick noticed the word *Nexus* printed on top.

'Don't be fooled or disenchanted by the cover,' Saul said, proffering the magazine for Nick's perusal. Said cover featured an imaginative illustration of a spaceship – like something from *Star Wars*. Underneath the spaceship was a circular pattern in a field of crops. 'Some of the stuff can be a little out there, but there's also a lot of science, too. Specifically*, fringe science*. A lot of speculation about the unexplained.'

Nick, who was especially *enchanted* with the cover – and with Saul's use of words – reached out to take the tendered magazine.

'Unexplained … you mean like ghosts?' he asked, fascinated despite himself. Nick's nightmares of shadowy beings, having reached a plateau the previous winter, showed no signs of abating. 'Ghosts and spirits that come from other worlds?'

'Occasionally,' said Saul, and tipped Nick a wink. 'But more often than not, the articles are about what you see on the cover. Unexplained things that fly around in terrestrial skies. Where they might come from; who or what might be piloting them. And this kind of alternative magazine tries to answer a lot of the questions people are too afraid to ask.'

Nick's eyes left the magazine and once more found the water. From this height, small boats and kayaks were visible, each speck trailing a white scud of spume. Then he sought the horizon ... a realm where clouds jostled, birds reeled, and a winter sun spangled them all.

'You're here looking for UFOs?' Nick asked, and laughed a little. It wasn't, he hoped, a skeptical laugh. 'Have you seen any?'

'A difficult question to answer,' Saul replied, gently prizing the magazine away from Nick's hands. 'A UFO, by definition, is an *unidentified* object, and I have certainly seen my fair share of those. All kinds of strange things floating in the clouds. Most people, young Nick, never take the time to stare up at the sky. And why not? Because their lives are so busy, of course. The only thing that seems to matter to anyone is what's immediately in front of them. So, my philosophy has always been that *somebody* has to do it. Somebody has to take notice of everything that goes *unnoticed*.'

After this, a lengthy discussion followed. Talk concerning Nick's sleep paralysis and the possibility of other life forms in the cosmos. Nicholas Ferris Wheeler, who had grown up having many deep-thinking exchanges with his teachers at school, would ultimately leave the slope that day convinced his encounter with Saul Kidman was the most enlightening of them all.

3

Nick returned to the cabin, furtively creeping on tiptoes through the kitchen. After the horror show of the morning, his imagination was working overtime, producing potential reprisals Wendy would mete out. In one of them, the entire Wheeler brood was gathered around the fireplace, warming their hands in preparation for an intervention which would see Nick grounded for the rest of his life. However, his fears proved unfounded. Nick managed to creep into his bedroom, unscathed. Bereft of Sebastian, his brother's unmade bed was also a cause for joy. If the tyrant wasn't in residence now, there was a good chance he was sleeping over at a friend's place.

Which meant Nick would be free of him for the rest of the evening.

But you're never completely free – not at night. There's still the boogeyman to contend with once you lay your head down on that pillow.

'Let's face it,' Nick said aloud, stepping out of his sneakers and flopping onto his bed. 'I'm past due for a boogeyman parade after the peace of the last few nights.'

Some of Saul's words from the previous afternoon came floating back.

Maybe these things you see aren't anything to be afraid of, Nick. Maybe they're just visitors from elsewhere trying to make contact with you.

Not likely. If this were the case, why were most Shadow creatures equipped with evil eyes and occasional snouts? Surely, that kind of physical get-up was a template for wickedness, no matter which universe you sprouted from ...

From the other room, Nick could make out the sound of his father's television set, the volume turned low but still loud enough for Nick to hear the voice of ALF coming through. ALF, the alien lifeform who devoured cats yet still found human allies to love him. By now, Wendy and Chad would know he was home ... but were too tired to care. Punishment, it seemed, could wait for another day.

As sleep settled, it was ALF's voice Nick heard

following him into his dreams. ALF had one furry arm outstretched, and he was telling Nick that aliens had nothing to do with his sleep dilemma at all ...

***

On his bed, Nick lay paralyzed.

He felt awake, but he knew he couldn't be … because an ominous shade of purple covered his bedroom. Like knuckled tree roots, dark shapes were crowded into the corners. The bedroom door (which Nick had closed before climbing into bed) was now open like a maw. Infusing the hallway was an even darker shade of purple. Knowing the effort would be futile, Nick tried to waggle his fingers and move his hip joints. Focusing attention on his feet, he also came up against the same roadblock; not so much as a minor movement from the pinky toe, whose nail had grown sharp.

It was during this interval Nick saw and felt the first fleeting movements of shadow, slithering denizens at the door.

Nick felt a flicker in his nervous system.

Located in his upper forearms, the sensation was delicate, but there was enough for movement; enough to propel him onto his elbows. Halfway out of his bed, Nick glanced down to find himself staring at his own body.

I've stepped out of it like a suit of clothes, he thought.

Until now, nothing approaching an out-of-body experience had featured into the mix.

Its inclusion brought on the first whisper of panic.

Stay cool. Think of this as a good thing. At least you're not completely helpless.

Studied in a mirror for twelve years, Nick's face, nestled in his pillow, looked different. Though all things were accounted for (the soft cheeks; the sweep of brown fringe), Nick saw hidden minutiae flaws, normally concealed. Fat blackheads stood out on his nose. His lower legs were crooked and thin. This was, he thought, like hearing your voice through a tape recorder. While you recognized the voice as your own, its timbre sounded poles apart from what you were used to.

Have my nostrils always been that big?

From the hallway came an ominous sound. Against his better judgement, Nick turned toward it. Though he no longer had a body, his awareness still moved like one. Away from the bed he travelled, moving with all the finesse of a ghost, into the purple-saturated hallway; its wooden floor decorated with a giant swath of afghan.

The sound, at first hard to determine, was revealed: bells, a clarion of them. It was a ringing containing a melody, as if some form of choir lay in wait outside the cabin.

Outside.

That's where he was headed: somewhere out in the open.

Past Wendy and Chad's room, he drifted – their door also open. Peering in, he was unsurprised to see his father's bed empty.

Because this isn't my world.

No … this was the world of the Shadows, where patriarchal stepmothers were cast aside for even darker creatures.

Creatures calling him out of his body.

What if I can never return?

Nick attempted to change course, but his struggles were in vain. Through the open front door, he floated; a firmament of stars awaited, their brilliance transforming the driveway into luminosity brighter than a noonday sun. Trees – high larches given life as a kind of rustic fencing – were taller here than their daylight siblings, serrated tops like jagged teeth. These alterations, ranging from minor to vast, were all the evidence Nick needed to concede he was far from home.

His path appeared. Following its coils and turns, Nick realized he was not alone in this journey.

Amidst the thickets, Shadows kept pace.

Predators abreast of prey.

Occasionally, they called out to each other, staccato whistle-like warnings. Some were up high, swinging from branches like a troupe of acrobats. Though Nick attempted to get a fix on their forms, they would dissolve before so much as a limb revealed itself.

Finally, the path ended, and Nick came to his slope in Deception Pass.

With the waters and sky revealed, so too were the Shadows, their penchant to hide wholly abandoned. On the same swath of land where Saul Kidman brooded and sky-watched, creatures were exposed in their dozens. While a few lounged in the manner of dogs, others cavorted like tigers. Seeing Nick approach, their actions became frenetic, moving in primitive thrall to an elegy only they could hear.

Emerging like an alpha male, the Hat Man appeared.

He wore a fedora as black as his body.

No matter how much preparation Nick afforded himself, the Hat Man shattered his every defense. Though eyeless, the Hat Man saw. Though featureless, the stark cut-out of his silhouette still conveyed malevolence. While Nick had never seen the suggestion of lips, there was little doubt the entity smiled: a stalwart grin germane to a serial prankster. Separated by a few feet, the Hat Man raised one dark hand and pointed it skyward.

Toward a firmament of moving stars rearranging their orbits.

Erupting in a sudden cacophony of sound, the Shadows howled at the boy, the moon, and their master.

Crowding together, the stars formed a simple sentence.

Bring another.

The Hat Man tittered.

His minions, in turn, also commenced chortling. The sounds, like vibrations flying through the air, contained a dirge impossible to tune out or silence. While there were human characteristics, the Shadows' mirth was more akin to the whooping of hyenas.

Bodiless, Nick could nevertheless feel the pull of flesh, an invitation to return home – these creatures had shared their message.

Like an afterimage, the words formed in the stars burned bright behind the veil of his vision.

Bring another.

4

Rosa Collins hated Saturdays.

In Deception Pass, every Saturday felt the same, just like the day before it. And the day before that. So, when every day was more or less the same, there was no reason to yearn for the weekend. Of course, things were different during the school year – but Whidbey Island had a languid rhythm all its own.

Part of it was Rosa's mother. For some reason, she could barely stand the faces of her children when Saturday approached.

No – there's a big reason. Her bottles of gin and tonic. Her tumbler glass filled with a mound of ice.

Rosa understood there was probably an aspect of shame that came from drinking in front of Mitchell and her.

'We're here in the middle of a winter wonderland, and the only thing you two want to do is stay inside and watch television. Well, I won't have it. Out, the both of you. Put on your snowshoes, go out, and play with the other kids.'

'There *are* no other kids,' Mitchell said. The riposte had been indulged so many times it now had the repetition of prayer. For his thirteen years, Mitchell was short. And saddled with a face bursting with so many pimples, it resembled a pie crust.

'There isn't a decent playground anywhere that's not completely covered in snow.'

'There's that Sabastian boy who lives a few houses over,' his mother told him. 'And that other one … what's his name?'

'Nicholas,' said Rosa, unable to quell the faraway look she got whenever she thought of him.

Her brother made a horrid face. 'You're talking about Ferris Wheel? He's stupid. A stupid weirdo. Everyone says so.'

'He is *not*,' said Rosa. 'Just because he keeps to himself –'

'Like he has a choice?'

'Quiet, both of you. I don't care what you do,

whether you play with the Wheelers or not. Just do it outside, where there's plenty of fresh air.'

'And barely any –'

'Sunshine. Yes, I've heard that before, too. Just keep walking, and you'll be warmed up in no time. Remember, your father bought this place for our holidays. So, there'll be no more television or Commodore 64 until Monday.'

At the mention of *Father,* Mitchell's recalcitrance vanished. Rosa also went silent, happy to fetch her coat from the rack, a gesture she had accepted her mother's decree.

Without stopping to invite her brother, Rosa quietly opened the front door and slipped out, mindful of the dozen concrete steps whose surface lay brittle with melting ice.

***

With no one to plow this portion of the street in December, the tarmac leading away from Rosa's house was barely visible. Not that it was much of a road during the summer, either … just a hollowed-out track. Using the high grass as her compass point, Rosa slowly navigated her way through a thoroughfare which would eventually link up with Campbell Lake. Far away from that direction, a cormorant followed a loon's scream … a bird's guttural singsong which often reminded Rosa of a pig.

My brother is the pig.

Yes, Mitchell assuredly was – although, his piggish traits had only come into being after Patrick Collins died. Patrick, a middle-aged father of two, had eaten the wrong kind of lasagna one night. Mitchell, a bright student who idolized his father, was ill-equipped to deal with his departure. Thereafter, he slipped into a pig-headedness of the first degree ... almost as if asshole genes were activated during his time of bereavement.

And yet – I turned out just fine.

Rosa loved her father. Yet, the core of her adoration did not come from some hero-worship sprung from his power and authority. No, it came from that secret place all daughters carried within them like a talisman. Patrick Collins was her *protector*. More, he exhibited no propensity for domestic competition like the morbid species of rivalry that mothers (including her own) were often known to embrace. When Patrick passed, a part of Rosa also died … but another part toughened, her previously naive view of the world molted like a second skin. Since then, the siblings had grown apart and any playtime away from the cabin now were entirely solo affairs.

***

Soon Campbell Lake revealed itself, its small island home to a lone fisherman. With no plan in place besides making it to the shore, Rosa halted, noticing the beach contained someone else … not an angler this time, but a person whose wiry frame was unmistakable.

Nicholas Wheeler (Ferris Wheel to those who knew him) stood perched on a sandbar, brazenly skipping rocks atop the lake's surface. Silhouetted against a cloud-shrouded sun, he appeared every inch the archetypal innocent.

Huck Finn for a new age, Rosa thought, and couldn't help but smirk. Though she knew Nick only peripherally – and had spoken to him all of three times – it wasn't rare to see him around the trails of Deception Pass. With his penchant for solitude, opportunities arose for Rosa to play the part of spy on more than one occasion. Her brother Mitchell had been right, of course – everyone who lived here thought Nicholas strange, bordering on bonkers. And yet, the opinion of others had done little to assuage Rosa's curiosity. It was *because* he was so strange that Rosa desired to know him. Desired even to

(touch his hair)

be his friend.

Despite a half-dozen efforts to engage him, the boy would invariably shy away. Either he didn't like girls, or he was suspicious of anybody showing kindness.

A lifetime of bullying was reason enough to be wary.

Maybe today would be different.

As she edged closer, Rosa could tell this wasn't to be the case: Nick's posture was like a pitcher about to release a fastball. Despite the cold, there was an accumulation of sweat on his brow. With the lapping waves and breeze masking her arrival, Rosa could also see his lips moving rapidly, mumblings aimed at the sky.

'Aim for that person on the island, fishing,' she said, raising her voice to be heard above the sound of wind. 'With some kind of far-off target, you're bound to have more luck.'

Nick froze mid-swing, almost tripping in the process. Jerking around to face the interloper, it was clear he'd not heard her approach, thinking himself alone. For a moment, the boy was all agitation and annoyance as though caught in the act of something forbidden. Then, seeing Rosa less of a threat, he visibly relaxed.

'And risk hitting him? Not worth the trouble.'

Rosa eyed the lone island-dweller: a grizzled man wearing red coveralls and at least eighty feet away. '*Hitting* him? No offense, Nick, but you couldn't make the distance. *Nobody* could.'

She had his full attention now; Nick studied her curiously through the mop of his brown fringe. He asked, 'How do you know my name?'

'Everybody does,' Rosa replied. 'I'm not sure if you've noticed, but during the winter, our phonebook has one page.'

Nick grunted, conceding the point. Though Rosa had hoped for a laugh.

'What are you doing out here?' she asked, hoping to penetrate his façade of indifference.

'Isn't it obvious?'

'No, I mean … doesn't matter. Did your parents kick you out, too? My mom hates me staying inside on Saturdays.'

Under Nick's full scrutiny, Rosa could feel herself becoming self-conscious … and hated herself for it. No boy her own age deserved to wield that kind of influence.

'You're Rosa? Rosa Collins?'

'That's right.'

'You live not far from here?'

'Equally right.'

'And you're a grade behind me, aren't you?'

'Yes … but we're the same age.'

Nick paused, diverting his attention once again to the coverall-wearing angler. Then he said, 'Your brother is a bully.'

Though her first instinct had always been to defend her own, Rosa decided to bite her tongue and let the remark go unanswered.

By not replying, she was granting validity to his statement.

This seemed to quell his initial frostiness. 'If it's any consolation, my brother is a bully, too. And I'm not just saying that because he rags on me. At school, I see him picking on some of the other kids, flicking their ears on the bus. Wendy doesn't want to hear it.'

'She's your stepmom, isn't she?'

Nick was nodding emphatically. 'My real mom died from a disease, obstructive sleep something. One night she went into cardiac arrest.'

Not about to correct Nick's error that such an illness was more likely a disorder, Rosa instead said, 'You can die from that in your *sleep*?'

Another vigorous shake of his head. 'It can happen. I was only seven.'

'Oh.'

There was more Rosa wanted to say. How her own father died in a manner that wasn't so dissimilar. And how this gave them equal footing. Not only for the orphan card, they also shared common ground with a mutual cause: permission to take up a rallying cry at the injustice of the universe itself.

'I have to go,' said Nick abruptly, brushing his trousers as though they were soddened with sand. 'My friend will be waiting for me.'

'Oh,' she repeated, struggling to put a face to Nick's mention of a friend. Just who was he alluding to? Someone else who vacationed on the island? Another girl? Although there *weren't* any other girls. Not during the weeks before Christmas. Unless …

'You're not talking about that old man, are you?'

Nick looked up at her sharply, his caught-in-the-act look returned. 'How do you … you know about Saul?'

'Yes, that's who he said he was when he stuck out his hand.'

'What do you mean?'

'I mean he tried to befriend *me* one day, not far from here.'

'I don't believe you.'

'It's true,' Rosa said. 'I saw him for the first time last year. Scaling cliff faces like a crazy person and dressed in a *suit*.'

Nick looked confused. 'A suit? We can't be talking about the same person.'

Rosa was nodding. 'Not just a suit, either. Once I saw him wearing suspenders, and another time after that I think he was wearing a cape. Only it wasn't a cape … it was more like something a priest would wear.'

'We're *definitely* not talking about the same person.'

'But you *did* say his name was Saul?'

A sudden and strong breeze rose up, buffeting them both and causing Rosa to shrink back and blow into her hands. Nick was looking back in the direction of his cabin … as if expecting Saul to sashay over the next rise at any moment.

After a protracted silence, Nick finally asked, 'What did he say to you? When you spoke to him.'

'He wanted to know my name. I wouldn't give it to him.'

'Why not?'

'A better question to ask would be *why*. We're young, Nick. Practically kids. Do you make a habit of talking to strange men when you're out walking on your own?' Around her cupped palm, Rosa laughed. 'Well, I guess you do. Because you said he's your friend.'

Nick was inching away from her now, slowly putting distance between them as though Rosa were suddenly contagious. When it became evident he had every intention of leaving, Rosa said, 'Hey, I'm sorry. I didn't mean it like that. I just think you need to be careful. That man … he didn't look proper. If you're going to see him, I'd like to come along with you.'

Nick had not stopped backtracking, the look on his face even more confused. 'Why would you do that? Not a minute ago you called him a crazy person.'

'To make sure you're going to be all right. And I didn't *say* he was a crazy person. I just said he was acting like one.'

For a long moment Nick said nothing, weighing his next course of action carefully. At last, with fatalistic import, he said, 'Saul is a brilliant man. You're just jealous because I know someone like him. You should go home … and please don't follow me.'

With that, Nick trotted away, steadily building into a gallop. Rosa made a half-hearted attempt to follow and gave up quickly, knowing it would be futile trying to catch up.

Minutes later, he vanished completely, the boy's sneaker prints in the perennial snow like a phantom calling-card.

***

Girls have a way of ruining everything, Nick thought as he scaled an outcropping and jumped back down again. He wasn't sure why he travelled

67

so far from home and his favorite slope

(the dream ... just admit your dream)

but running into Rosa Collins was not anticipated or altogether welcomed. Sure, she was pretty (one could even argue the word beautiful applied), yet good looks did not undermine all the other aspects girls carried around with them. First, they were bossy. Second, nosy. And having the nerve to lecture him about somebody she didn't *know* was all the proof Nick required. Girls like Rosa were a bother best avoided.

Never trust a ginger, Sebastian once declared when referencing their neighbors. *Especially a whole family of them.*

Rosa's brother and mother were also redheads; copper tufts budded from their bulky winter parkas like flaming matchsticks. Exactly *why* Sebastian thought redheads were treacherous was anybody's guess. Perhaps he would ask him later when –

'Nick, there you are.'

For the second time today, Nick was caught off guard. Once again, he almost stumbled ... yet managed to stay upright at the last moment. In front of him ran a small weathered bridge linking Nick's present footpath with another.

Saul Kidman stood on the bridge.

'I didn't mean to startle you,' said Saul. Today, the old man wore a dark trench coat, its sides lined with a dozen pockets. Wet snow clung to the hems. 'You looked like you were in a world of your own just now.'

'I was,' Nick replied, wondering where Saul had sprung from. One minute, Nick had been sure the way ahead was clear. And then …

'Just wool-gathering, I suppose.'

'It's certainly a fine day for it. As crisp and clear as a chandelier. What are you doing so far away from our slope? I thought we agreed to meet there again.'

For a fleeting second, Rosa's words came back; Rosa distrusted all strangers on sight. *That man, he didn't look proper.*

But what constituted proper? After all, Saul was just a man … despite his interest in all things mysterious. And all men were basically the same underneath, weren't they?

Nick said, 'We did. I was on my way there just now. Earlier, I wanted to go for a long walk, shake off last night. I … had some dreams again. Bad ones.'

No part of this statement was untrue. Those words the stars had spelled out, like a gross invitation …

At this, Saul brightened, his concern of Nick's whereabouts abruptly forgotten. With one arm, he motioned Nick forward. 'I'm so sorry to hear that.

Do you want to talk about it? Pain shared is pain halved, Nick. I truly believe that.'

Of course, Nick *did* want to talk about it. Last night's dream, or episode, had been an important one. Though Rosa Collins had planted a real thread of uncertainty concerning Saul Kidman, he was still the only person on earth ready to lend an attentive ear. Kindness and compassion on his part counted for something in a world that had shown Nick little of either.

Pain shared is pain halved, Nick.

Managing a genuine smile, Nick stepped up onto the bridge.

5

With dusk approaching, the entity named Saul Kidman watched as the boy disappeared. First the back of his head, and then his tracks in the snow swallowed up by a strong wind.

Tonight, a storm was in the offing.

One that might potentially force him to seek shelter. In the caves, Saul could use the time to take sustenance from the darkness.

And seek counsel.

Should his master consent to it.

It was a difficult life, this existence as Saul. Difficult and unbearably long. Human beings, never knowing a proper purpose, were not the only species to feel abandoned by their creator. Such a condition (forever unreconciled to a greater whole) applied to many creatures.

Even to those who weren't human.

How many nights had Saul lain awake thinking of this puzzle? That he, a thing sprung from darkness, was essentially a being who shared humanity's traits. And while Saul's life was measured in centuries, he had pondered this enigma when Homo sapiens were only a bourgeoning species along the Cascade Range.

Created in their image – yet belonging to a different tribe.

Today, Nicholas Wheeler imparted new findings, the boy's latest vision during his sleep paralysis. Not only had there been another appearance by the Hat Man, but Nicholas walked this very slope. After, the stars passed on their brazen instructions. This confession, like most of Nick's admissions, was in no way revelatory.

Because Nick was divulging things Saul already knew.

Once upon a time, he had been *similar* to the Shadows of Nick's nightmares. Cavorted as they did, unencumbered by flesh.

Yet their eternal method for intrusion into *this* world – the doorway of human sleep – had proven itself time and again through the generations to be limited in scope. So, a new strategy was forged, one whose outcome might free them to interact completely unfettered by borders …

By creating me.

This was why he brooded now, and why the madness of soliloquy and introspection (qualities he'd once thought only the human animal vulnerable to) came upon him as they did: dusk had a way of sharpening this emotion into despair.

The night was a time when creatures of darkness were just as susceptible to malaise as any other living thing born with blood between its ears.

Through no will of his own, Saul Kidman had been guided to Nicholas Wheeler. Saul was glad of the pairing. His master considered the boy special, and Saul could see why: Nicholas was not like other children; he burned with an imagination that could potentially bridge worlds, dogmas, and more.

Power to unmake belief systems already in place.

This was why it was important for the boy to believe in mysteries. Exposure to Saul's world of strangeness (not solely in the sky but everywhere) provided musculature to minds begging to be molded; gave them an evolutionary nudge to begin great works.

While Saul did not wholly understand their relationship with Nick, he comprehended the fundamentals of his own mission. His education only beginning, Nick needed further grooming. By passing on portions of his own knowledge, Saul was securing a boarding pass back into the promised land the Shadows called home.

Once returned, Saul would slough off his unwanted humanity, once and for all.

Things had been going to plan.

But outside forces were prepared to arbitrate his efforts.

Like the girl child.

Despite failing to seduce Rosa the previous winter – she was a cunning intellect who somehow managed to see through the greater portion of his glamor – Saul was not overly concerned. Young Nicholas, detailing her misgivings today, had unwittingly ensured any threat she presented could be met head on.

With seed-sowing of his own, Rosa Collins' meddling could be thwarted before it began.

Knowing this, Saul felt his melancholy lift. Yes, he was a creature at the whim of this environment, prone to the sufferings that came with the flesh. But his condition was temporary. Soon would come a day when night no longer loomed as a peril; soon, it would be something to embrace and be made indivisible from.

Caught in the crosshairs of its own finite existence, beleaguered by another world beyond their own, the human species wasn't so fortunate.

***

Snow levels rose in Deception Pass, and so did the overall optimism in Nick's household. While it served as a physical indicator Christmas Day was fast approaching – a time when sibling grievances were temporarily thrust aside – it also served to transform the playing potential of the Wheelers' property. Idle for most of November, swing-sets and slides got a sudden work out. One of the roofs used to cover the three ATVs became, with the aid of piled snowdrift, a practical diving board in which to make snow-angels. Sebastian, having received a remote-controlled Jet Hopper as a birthday present the year before, decided to use the ice in the backyard to construct a makeshift track.

Even going so far as to enlist Nick's help in the planning and design.

Despite being given no permission to race the machine, Nick reveled in the process, his penchant for design being given a worthwhile outlet. Louise, never outdone in any undertaking, was tasked with overseeing the tracks' visual aesthetic; she created stadium seating, crude advertising signs, and even a pit-lane fashioned from cardboard. Chad Wheeler, watching things unfold with Wendy from behind a small window in the laundry, was quick to claim credit for the children's sudden solidarity.

'And you didn't think the Jet Hopper was a good idea,' he said, squinting from the appearance of a winter sun through parting clouds. 'You said a remote-controlled car would go inside his closet faster than the golf clubs and karate uniform.'

Wendy said, 'I stand corrected.'

She was happy to indulge her husband for the day. Not for long, though. Her period was imminent, and with its arrival, restrained niceties would cease.

'Maybe if we bought Nick one, he might take an interest in cars, do you think? Potentially drive him away from those silly magazines and the company of old men?'

'Potentially,' said Chad. Though staring at Nick now (the boy was sitting on one end of a seesaw, bent over wads of paper like a mad scientist), he had grave reservations. No cars would be in the boy's future, remote or otherwise. There was even a chance he would turn out queer, a theory his more booze-addled acquaintances had been fond of floating on the rare occasions Wendy decided to throw a cocktail party for his faculty network.

I've noticed your boy likes to wear skivvies, Chad remembered Geoff Packman saying. *That doesn't qualify him for the ass-bandit brigade yet –*

but it might. Keep an eye on him, Chad. Maybe take him out hunting next time you're going up to Whidbey; otherwise, you'll have a faggot on your hands before you can blink.

***

By lunchtime, the track was completed. Sebastian declared the project an absolute success. Equipped with chicanes, hairpins, and a main straightaway dug out with a hoe (the rest required no more than a basic shovel), Louise wanted to know what the track would be called.

'Every circuit in the Formula One has one,' she said. 'A name.'

Sebastian brandished his Jet Hopper in one hand as if to emphasize his next words. 'Does this *look* like a Grand Prix car? It's an off-road buggy.'

'Whatever it is, we should test it out,' Nick said. 'There's no snow forecasted for the rest of the day, but you never know if –'

'Oh no. Now it's *we*, is it? This is *my* Jet Hopper. Dad and Mom bought it for *me*.'

Nick shrank back. Though, it wasn't because of Sebastian's assertion the car belonged to him. It was the reference to their stepmother as *Mom*. Perhaps the first occasion he'd done so. The first time *any* of them had. How had it come to this, Nick wondered.

A matriarch inserting herself into the family vocabulary.

With the thought, a sudden and morbid image sprang to life: Kayla Wheeler, literally rolling over in her coffin, puffs of dust and sods of dirt disturbed by the movement.

'She's not –' Louise began.

'It doesn't matter,' Sebastian said, realizing his Freudian slip and backtracking. 'Dad bought it for me, so I get to test it. Ferris Wheel, where are the batteries?'

But Nick only continued to retreat, knowing his work was done for the day. Now it was time to become invisible again, the third wheel whose services were no longer required.

***

Minutes later, he was back on his private path, the words from his dream like a pest that couldn't be dislodged.

Bring another …

When the cryptic arrangement first appeared, Nick had immediately known their import.

There had been no moment of confusion weighing the message through the eyes of his corporeal self.

Nick sensed the message had come directly

from the Hat Man.

Bring another, instead of you, that leering no-face proclaimed. Chaperone them into our waiting hands, and we'll leave you alone to go about your life.

An ultimatum from creatures that might not exist.

They're real, Nick thought. *You can't think they're not. It's like Saul says, even if nobody else can see the Shadows, that's only because they haven't been given any special sight.*

'As soon as I begin thinking they're make-believe,' Nick whispered. '*That's* when I let them in.'

The Hat Man's motives, though mysterious, did not feel like a big mystery.

Because in every parable Nick was aware of, devils and demons desired such bargains.

Give me another soul – and we'll leave yours alone.

Walking in a portion of condensed Douglas firs, Nick heard the crack of something trodden underfoot. A stick, perhaps. Tensing, he surveyed both path and boulders. Ahead lay a snow-dappled scree. Yesterday, Saul had frightened him, taking Nick completely unaware. Was Saul out here again today, away from his hillock and hotdogs?

Louder, the sound repeated.

Small rocks being displaced.

Through the trees ahead, something airborne whizzed past, only to land a few feet away. Heart thudding, Nick whimpered.

A hand reached out and cupped his shoulder.

'*Boo*!' came a girl's voice, and suddenly Rosa Collins was standing in front of him, her cheeks reddened by the elements and a gleeful gleam in her eyes.

'Scared you good and proper, didn't I? You should see your face.'

'You didn't scare me.'

But she had. And badly. In time with Nick's thudding heart, blood pounded through his ears.

'It's not funny,' he said. 'You shouldn't sneak up on people like that. I almost turned around and hit you.'

A small lie. But one he could live with. Instead of striking his would-be assailant, Nick had been on the cusp of fleeing pell-mell into the forest.

For a moment, Rosa's bravado crumpled; evidence such a prank wasn't within her usual scope of style.

Brightening, Rosa stuck out her hand. 'I'm sorry, really. But you'll live. Friends, Ferris Wheel?'

Nick regarded her jadedly. 'Please don't call me that. I hate it.'

Rosa frowned, puzzled. 'You do? I just thought … never mind. What do you prefer, anyway? I'll call you Nicholas, if you'd like.'

'Nick is fine,' he replied, momentarily awestruck at the girl's proximity. Of course, he was up-close with girls at school all the time. But it wasn't often they stared at you with their undivided attention. Rosa's hair – an auburn cast of red that was almost gold – clung to her brow in dainty half-moons.

Her eyes were the emerald-hue of shamrock.

She grew aware of his study and averted her eyes. Before more awkwardness could ensue, he asked, 'What are you doing out here, anyway? Did your mom kick you out of the house again?'

Rosa's reply was matter of fact. 'I came to see you. I know where you're headed but thought you might like to do something different today. Thought you'd like to see something *really* cool.'

'You're trying to stop me from seeing my friend again, aren't you?'

'I'm not trying to stop you from doing anything, Nick. Is there a rule that you have to hang out with that old guy all the time?'

'No, but –'

'So, what's stopping you from coming with me and doing something different?'

He was on the edge of another righteous reply,

but the forthright nature of Rosa's question stumped him. Because there was *nothing* stopping him from doing whatever he wanted. School holidays were in effect, and Christmas was just around the corner. If he wanted to take his shirt off and parade half-naked through the snow, not even Wendy could prevent it from happening.

'This cool thing … what is it?'

Rosa's full-fledged smile returned, a knowing lilt at the corners.

'Something nobody knows about except me.'

***

With Rosa leading, they took a southern trail; one even cruder and less trampled than Nick's. Here, the steep incline of hills blotted out even a rumor of the sea.

As they walked, Nick asked, 'Were you following me before? I don't think I've ever seen another person on that path.'

'I was,' Rosa replied, keeping her head forward. 'How else was I going to sneak up on you?'

Nick had no answer to this and could only stare at her back, mystified. *No gloves on today*, he thought. *She must be freezing.*

Had he recalled reading somewhere that girls

weren't as sensitive to cold as boys? Different body temperatures, or something. Or was it the other way around? Suddenly, as if in answer, the temperature seemed to plummet with a dramatic increase of wind.

Rosa asked, 'Have you ever been this way before?'

'No.'

'I'm taking us to where there used to be a lot of quarry caves. Most of them are sealed up now. Too dangerous for anybody but bats.'

'There are *bats*?'

Nick watched as the back of Rosa's head bobbed up and down. 'Of course. But they're hibernating this time of year. Mitchell says kids used to explore the caves, so they put steel bars over most of the entrances. Only they're designed in a way so there's enough room for the bats to slip through.' She cackled. 'Genuine *bat caves* right here in Deception Pass.'

Kids like us, Nick thought. About to voice his concern, Rosa said, 'The one we're going to has *no* bars, though. There's nothing blocking the way inside.'

So that was the ultimate destination.

A dangerous cave carved into the hills.

***

They came to the cave through a tree-studded grotto which led down to a small weir. The water was brackish, clotted with piles of refuse and chunks of floating ice.

'I thought nobody knows about this place except you,' said Nick.

'They don't.'

'Then why the rubbish? People, most likely older kids, have been using this spot.'

Ignoring him, Rosa was in the process of navigating the rocks surrounding the weir like a flotilla of icebergs, using them as steppingstones. Only a lesion of darkness before, Rosa's cave became fully illuminated: an oblate recess about fifteen-feet tall and ten across. While most of the protruding rocks were carved from decades of extreme weather along this crag, there was little doubt the cave was manmade. Nick could see supporting timber pylons the closer they got.

'What was this used for?' he asked, feeling the first thread of unease. So far, the journey had been smooth sailing ... yet the imminence of entering a dark and cramped space was now a humble reality.

'Everyone seems to have a different theory,' Rosa said. 'My mom says that during World War II, Japanese-American prisoners were flown over from the internment camps in Colorado and put to work around here. The caves were hollowed out for mining rocks, a kind of chain-gang thing. Mitchell thinks they were probably just regular prisoners, come down from Walla Walla.'

As if hesitant to go further, Rosa stopped at the entrance. 'If you can call murderers and rapists *regular* prisoners,' she added.

Having hurdled the final rocks, Nick came abreast his guide.

'You okay?'

'Fine,' he replied, though he was beginning to feel far from it.

'You're out of breath.'

Conscious of his stomach, Nick also noticed the ragged wheeze of his breathing. Relegated to physical education class once a week as his only sporting activity, overall fitness (or brandishing any muscle, for that matter) might forever be beyond his reach.

I don't think Rosa cares. Not going by the way she's looking at you.

Reserving her core attention for his hair, Rosa proceeded to study Nick's chin and neck. Once again feeling shy, he broke the weird connection.

From the depths of the cave came a sound.

'Please tell me that was the wind.'

'Of course, it was,' replied Rosa, and advanced inside. 'The old quarries are full of shafts that probably go on for miles. What say we take a look around and find out?'

The sound came again: escaping air – rich, low, and altogether unpleasant.

'You can't be serious? What if the bats are still in residence?'

Rosa tittered, the sound echoing. 'It's *bats* you're worried about?'

Other things existed in the dark besides flying vampires, and Nick knew of them intimately.

I'm wide awake – not in my bed. There's nothing out here in the real world that can hurt me.

But was this absolutely true? Lately, Nick had observed strange things with Saul. Things that shared space with this winter world of darkness and heights.

'Come on,' Rosa said, her back and gloveless hands already a receding smudge. 'Maybe we'll luck out and discover it's the lair of a superhero.'

***

With little light to guide them, Nick and Rosa descended into almost complete darkness before another light, its source elusive, paved the way ahead. Below, stalagmite protrusions were a hindrance, but enough remnants of a faux path remained to navigate without tripping over them.

Nick, not wanting to be seen as cowardly by

voicing any further objection to this excursion, remained silent until the strange light intensified.

'There must be an underwater stream in here,' he said.

On the rock walls, shimmering arcs of light were soon joined by the sound of rushing water.

'Makes sense,' Rosa said. 'We're probably being led straight to a sea cave.'

They were a feature of the island Nick knew little about – Sebastian often talked of kayaking through grottos during warmer weather. Imposing from the outside, Nick had given little thought to what lay on their *inside*.

More water, he supposed.

Bottomless pools of it.

When Nick and Rosa came upon the stream, however, it was disproportionately small compared to the sound it produced.

Staring at the rippling surface, Rosa said, 'We could almost skip across it.'

'We could,' Nick agreed, transfixed by surroundings becoming more lucid by the moment. Clearer, Nick noted, not from the light source coming from the mouth of the stream, but by the natural acclimation of their eyes to the darkness.

Opaque only moments ago, rocks on the other side of the water were now startling transparent.

'Look,' Nick said, and pointed. 'Is that ...?'

'Another tunnel? I think it is.'

If the one through which they'd entered appeared manmade, then this was its opposite: a maw transformed by elements and time. Smaller, its width appeared scorched, as if something had scoured through the sediment to create it.

'A cave *within* a cave,' Rosa said, already canvassing the edge of the stream for a launch point. 'Now this, I did not expect.'

Despite his fear of being perceived as craven, Nick couldn't help but voice misgivings. The stream could be deep, he cautioned, in which case Rosa ran the risk of being swept out to sea.

Nick was on his fourth complaint when Rosa let out a grunt of effort. Turning around, he observed her lunging across a warped portion of water not unlike his recently devised racing chicane. Then she was on the other side, stumbling a little with her arms outstretched to cushion a fall that never came.

'Your turn,' Rosa said, without turning around.

Nick, before attempting to jump, found a makeshift tree branch and – with the deftness of someone versed in science – proceeded to depth test. Kneeling for the task, the stench of the cave was overwhelming. A combination of marine matter and basement dank. Lest hesitation delay him, he pressed the stick into the current and felt the upmost relief when the tip encountered solid ground.

Less than two feet deep, give or take.

'Hurry up,' Rosa called over. Facing away from him, her attentions were reserved solely for their new find. 'Otherwise, I'm going in without you.'

Nick released the stick and watched as it was snatched away by the stream.

She's just teasing, he thought. *No way she'll go in alone.*

But already, the girl's back was disappearing into the murk.

Standing up ... Nick leapt abruptly, his feet colliding with solid ground. Like Rosa, he briefly faltered, locked in a precarious tightrope dance.

'You look scared enough to crap,' Rosa said, smiling.

Silence ensued before laughter erupted, the natural and tension-breaking kind. Nick, whose character was given to a serious bent, embraced the sound. With Wendy's dictatorship over his life a constant, absurdity and fun were often in short supply. Well, not today. Today, he would attempt some semblance of joy. If only for the girl standing next to him.

When the laughter abated, Rosa said, 'My brother, Mitchell, calls diarrhea *mud butt*.'

And they were off again, Rosa leaning on Nick

for support this time.

'We should come back with a flashlight. There's no point going in if we can't see anything.'

'There *is* light all around us,' Rosa said, and began making headway again. 'But I can't make out where it's coming from?'

She was correct. A radiance – like the faint ember of something quartz – strafed the ceiling. Perhaps this was all they were observing: a cavern lined by naturally occurring quartz rock.

Behind them, the sound of rushing water began to dissipate, the dimensions of the cavity becoming more prominent. An expanse of ceiling (something only glimpsed moments ago) now rose to giddy heights, a scaffolding of scarps and outcroppings.

'All of this ... reminds me of Snowy's mouth,' Rosa said.

'Snowy?'

'Our cat. Stupid name, I know. Mitchell's idea. All this is like the inside of his mouth.'

It was a strange thing to say ... yet Nick had little trouble understanding what Rosa meant. Like protruding spines, there were ridges everywhere, a vast catalogue of the sharp and sculpted. The further they walked, the grimier the light became, illuminating additional paths and tunnels. Nick's unease, not fully experienced since spotting the original opening, began to ripen.

'Stop,' he said, and Rosa did just that. 'I think we should go back.'

Something in Nick's voice piqued Rosa's concern. 'What's bothering you?'

Surprised at the words tumbling out, yet unable to halt them, Nick said, 'I know people talk about me. Not just kids at school but everyone living here. There are rumors about me, aren't there?'

'Nick –'

'That I have some kind of sickness? That I have really bad nightmares?'

Even in the gloom, Nick detected an awkward change in Rosa's deportment.

People were talking, all right.

Nick said, 'I've heard them all, believe me. That I'm a serial bed wetter, and that's the real reason my parents wanted to send me to the hospital. That I sleepwalk. The truth is, I *still* experience night terrors, so that part's true. But there's much more to it.'

He was divulging secrets only uttered in the presence of his family or Saul. Expecting remorse, Nick was pleased to feel something different: simple relief. Spilling the goods to a grandfatherly figure was one thing; sharing them with a girl his own age gave the affliction less of a taboo quality.

Rosa asked, 'Why are you telling me this now?'

'Because I don't want to go any further. If you knew what it's like for me ...'

'What *is* it like for you?'

Nick was on the verge of giving Rosa a crash course on the minutiae of paralysis when a sound (this one having little to do with wind) drifted out from the belly of the cave.

'That *wasn't* a breeze,' Rosa said.

'No.'

'What do you think it was?'

'Someone else is down here.'

He wished for a better way to frame it. What Nick heard had been commotion; a group of people amassed.

'There's nothing on the surface but forest and other cabins,' Rosa said.

'So, where's it coming from?'

Despite Nick's objection, they both began moving again. With every step, the girth of the passageway seemed to widen. Filaments of light, like the reflection of mirrors, abruptly bled into rock.

Rosa asked, 'Do you smell that?'

Nick could. Though it was a scent far removed from briny water and moldy cellars.

'Like a county fair?' he ventured. But that wasn't quite right, either. A fair entailed things like funnel cakes and the suggestion of cow crap. This was more like its greasy cousin. Had he caught its scent before? Nick thought he had.

Though *never* this strong.

'Rosa,' Nick said, suddenly struggling to get words out. If the atmosphere in the cave was oppressive before, it was doubly so now. A clinging miasma. 'We have to turn around and go back.'

Glamor lay in the air ahead, and Rosa had caught the aroma. While the environment remained unpleasant, it also had a mysterious undercurrent: of a road untraveled by anything or anybody else.

***

Rock escarpments were beginning to move with the roiling precision of a wave. Beneath Nick's feet, regular dirt had taken on the rigidity of glass, a brown surface changed to black; its momentum having the urgency of an escalator. And their physical selves were also about to undergo a metamorphosis – jackets and trousers becoming less substantial by the moment. A few paces ahead, Rosa was beginning to sense the panic of their plight. Turning around, she shouted something, but her words were drowned by the steadily thickening air.

So, you've come to me in daylight, Nick thought now, his declaration aimed at creatures who only appeared in dreams. *What have you got for me, then?*

A lot, it would seem. The walls, now dissolved, presently revealed a blighted landscape, one stretching into the distance.

A landscape of glass.

Visible on the horizon, rectangular structures strafed an alien sky.

'What's happening?' he heard Rosa cry out, some portion of clarity returning. 'Where *are* we?'

***

As the new landscape came into focus, so too did their physical selves. Rosa, no longer some cartoon arrangement, stood against a backdrop of tenebrous sky. Faraway edifices also became more concrete, their outer façades exposing windows and rooftops beholden to spires. Nick, having only ever skated the periphery of this world, was aware on some fundamental level he was now reconciled with it wholly. For her part, Rosa was doing well. Reaching out, she grasped Nick's hand in a gesture of alliance.

Nick grasped her back.

'What you were saying before about your nightmares?'

'That there was more to them than regular

nightmares.'

'Is this some of that more?'

'I think so. We should keep moving. The ground … it doesn't feel solid.'

Still linked, they began walking. Rosa, sneaking furtive glances over her shoulder, was perhaps hoping their entry point would reappear. Ahead lay the peculiar buildings which gave them a rudimentary compass point ... if not a destination.

'Are you dreaming now?' Rosa asked. 'Are we? How can we be here, Nick?'

Nick pinched the soft flesh of Rosa's palm, a touch to answer her question.

'When I sleep, I wake up unable to move. I'm basically paralyzed. And *nothing* snaps me out of it. I can sometimes move my eyes, but only just. The rest of my body is like I'm dead. What I see when I open my eyes ... is not quite the real world. Everything looks the same, but it's not. It's different.'

Rosa didn't reply at first, only studied the distant buildings. Then she said: 'Is *this* that somewhere different?'

'Maybe. But I'm not paralyzed; I'm walking around in my real body. And you're here with me. Which means Saul was right. I'm not crazy.'

At the mention of Saul's name, Nick expected some kind of retort. But Rosa had eyes only for the heavens. Their clouds, a strange arrangement of orange-tipped cumulus, churned with a motion far stranger than any Nick had glimpsed above the weirs of Deception Pass.

***

'There's more,' he told Rosa. 'When I'm paralyzed and can't move, I *see* things.'

They were standing in something akin to a street, black glass underneath their toes like a reflective river. Close now, the strange buildings were a jumbled architecture of material not germane to Nick's world at all. Like Silly Putty, he thought. Shaped together by a giant's hand. Above, the burnt-orange clouds continued to churn, their bottoms hiding a deluge in the making.

'What do you see?' Rosa asked.

'*Shadows*,' Nick replied. 'Shadows that are somehow alive. When I was younger, there wasn't much shape to them, and I didn't know if they were good or bad. Or if they were animals or people. Now, I think, they're probably neither. I think they're something … in between. Like this place.'

Nick's words, perhaps serving as a catalyst, caused sudden motion from between the buildings – a flitting of presences. Of course, he'd known this moment was imminent ... but hoped to delay its arrival.

Instead, his words acted as a summons.

Ushering dark shapes from the culverts.

***

Like a legion of wraiths, they emerged; sinuous at first, then slowly gaining bulk. Again, with that unconscious tendency, Nick seized Rosa's hand, astonished he possessed the ability to move. Although free during his last encounter, Nick had been a wandering spirit, his mind untethered.

'I'm sorry, Rosa,' Nick said. 'You should have stayed far away from me.'

Her reply was urgent. 'What happens when you dream, Nick? How do you wake yourself up?'

I don't, he almost replied. But was that true? Usually it took an episode to reach its climax before Nick could wrestle himself back to a semblance of true consciousness. At the last moment, when the creatures reached out to *touch* him, there would often come a boiling point. And yet ... surely this wasn't the only avenue of escape?

A tugging on his sleeve. With the sensation came a roiling sound: a dirge of Shadow throats.

First, they were an agitated mass advancing across the glass, then a pack with limbs. Jostling, their movements became frenetic.

Moments went by as Nick simply stared, his mounting trepidation replaced with curiosity. Coupled together, their bodies in a shifting state of flux, it was easy to imagine these creatures as alien lifeforms, recently hatched and knowing only a primitive need to feed.

'*Nick.*'

Breaking the paralysis, Rosa jerked Nick by the arm. At long last, he turned and sprinted. Rosa, also running, snatched terrified glances in their wake. Building speed, the air commenced to change once again, a bourgeoning of familiar color. Seeing this, their run became a haphazard dash.

Catching scent of their imminent escape, the Shadows were in a further state of transformation: teeth branching out from anatomies, becoming more organic with every inch covered.

6

In Deception Pass, two households warred. Both children, having returned in a state of disarray, would not give up their secrets easily. Parting ways after their narrow escape from the tunnel, Nick attempted to swear Rosa into secrecy, knowing any blame for her distress would be heaped upon the strange boy named Ferris Wheel ... a boy prone to sleepwalking and nightmares. Rosa had agreed. But how could she endeavor to hide her tousled hair and a face so red it looked frostbitten?

'You're not telling me something,' her mother said, the gin bottle out for the weekend; Chrissie Collins already two olive-adorned glasses down. 'It was just a matter of getting lost for a little while?

Mmhmm. I don't believe that for a second, young lady. You know Whidbey Island even better than your other home.'

Her mother was right. In all their years frequenting these cold roads, Rosa prided herself on her keen sense of direction.

'The tunnels,' Rosa said, hoping a sliver of truth would mitigate her mother. 'They were my idea. I wanted to explore one, in particular. We went in too far and had a hard time finding our way back.'

'I've expressly forbidden you to go *anywhere* near those. What were you thinking?'

'I wasn't, obviously. I wasn't thinking. Nick –'

'It was really his idea, wasn't it? That's a troubled boy, Rosa. So, Mitchell tells me. You shouldn't play with someone like that. Wait until his parents receive a call from me.'

'You wouldn't?'

'I would,' Chrissie stated, sipping her gin in tandem with controlled bursts of pacing. 'Don't think I won't. What are you hiding? Just look at the state of you.'

Rosa didn't reply, only stared at the carpet, her expression guilty and forlorn. How could she possibly answer *that* question with any truth?

***

For Nick, things were even more unpleasant. Wendy, having taken Chrissie's call as a pretext to implement punishments already in waiting, relegated Nick to his room with no avenue of escape. Even Sebastian was not permitted to enter, his younger brother in quarantine for the foreseeable future. From outside the door came familiar sounds: Nick's stepmother in the throes of a tantrum while Chad cowered before the tiger like a dog baring its belly in surrender.

'This is the last straw, Chad. I've had it up to here with him. First, Nick's fraternizing with a creepy old man; now, he's corrupting other children with his fantasies.'

'Wendy, please keep it down. He'll hear you.'

'I don't give a shit what he hears. The boy is twelve and behaves like he's five. When are you going to wake up and see Nick for what he truly is?'

This was a new one in Wendy's arsenal. And what did it mean, exactly? Could she sense in some fundamental way Nick's corruption? Did Nick carry the stink of Shadows with him after every encounter?

'The boy is troubled. I admit that. Perhaps this place is no good for him. Perhaps it's time to take him back home.'

Like Rosa, Nick had been unable to hide his dread upon returning, sure in the knowledge his demons had a window into his everyday life and could now appear, without warning, at the drop of a hat. If an underground tunnel could materialize as a gateway into their world, then why not an ordinary door attached to a house? Why not a hole in the ground?

And what did Rosa say? How much did she tell?

The answer came shortly after with a quiet knock to the bedroom door. Strangely enough, it was Louise making a rare appearance. Today, his sister wore a white blouse and red beret, the outfit giving her the dour look of an old dame from one of her favorite mystery novels.

'Your friend says she saw something with you in the cave,' Louise said, closing the door silently and then placing herself at the foot of Nick's bed. 'Something strange. She's scared out of her wits.'

'What did she see?'

'Why don't you tell me? Maybe I can try to calm Wendy down if you tell me the truth.'

Nick fidgeted, his memory of the Shadow city and its glass horizon still sharp. What would Nick and Rosa have seen if they'd decided to enter a building? Did the underling Shadows call those walls home? No, Nick had the impression something higher-up and darker dwelled there ...

'Nothing,' Nick said. 'We saw nothing. I was

telling Rosa about some of my nightmares, and she got spooked, wigged out. We were walking around in the dark. I guess Rosa has a vivid imagination.'

'That's what Wendy was afraid of,' Louise said. 'She thinks you're infecting other children. She even used that word. Infecting.'

I probably am, Nick thought. *Perhaps just knowing about the Shadows opens their world to you.*

It was a frightening notion – something Saul might have communicated had he been present to hear Nick's sorry tale. Well, he'd be hearing about it soon enough. If not from the lips of the town, then from Nick himself.

Saul will know what to do. Saul will have answers.

'I have to go,' Louise said. 'I'm not supposed to be in here.'

'Why?' Nick asked his sister, the question having nothing to do with her reasons for leaving. 'Why does she hate me so much? What did I ever do to her?'

As if echoing Wendy's spiel, Louise said, 'It's nothing you've *done*, Nick. It's what you are. What you represent. All us original Wheelers. We're the offspring of another woman, and she *hates* that. You, especially, are easy to intimidate. But you learn to live with it. We have to. Because our father is never going to leave her.'

***

Though Nick's first instinct was to escape again, he knew doing so would only invite Wendy's further wrath. Finding Saul again was paramount, but Saul would have to wait. For the time being, the best thing Nick could do was stay unseen and quiet. Chad, anticipating his son's decision, poked his head through the door later that night.

'We're going into town early tomorrow. For shopping. When we get back, we're going to talk. And if I were you, I'd use the time to think long and hard about what you're going to say.'

'Dad –'

'Not now. Tomorrow. I don't want you going outside again, either. Even to work on Sebastian's track.' Chad hesitated, as if his next question brought with it significant guilt. 'Have you been sleeping okay this week?'

'Fine,' Nick murmured in reply, only wanting his father to disappear. He didn't care; none of them did. Giving voice to any truths in this exchange would not postpone any punishments lying in wait.

'Just fine?' As if sensing the lie, Chad hung around for a moment, a wedge of light from the living room making a stark pattern on Nick's carpet.

Then he pulled the door shut firmly, disappearing down the hallway.

**

What drew Nick to the phone the next morning he couldn't say – feelings of betrayal topped the list. His recent experience, though terrifying, had been a *shared* experience. One where Rosa Collins had also taken the brunt of something otherworldly. Traditionally, allies were often forged this way. So, what had been the reason forcing Rosa to buckle and confess?

Standing in the kitchen, Nick recalled his conversation the previous week: Rosa's declaration that Whidbey Island took up one page of the phonebook during the winter. She'd been right, of course; Nick found Rosa's household on the third line of the telephone directory Wendy kept in a drawer.

While it was more likely either her mother or Mitchell would answer, Rosa picked up on the fifth ring.

'Is that you, Nick? What time is it?'

Rosa sounded even worse than Nick felt, her usually soft voice cracked.

'It's me. I said yesterday that you should have stayed away from me. Now I'm beginning to think it's *me* that should have stayed away from *you*.'

'Nick, you have every right to be angry. But I had no idea my mother would make the call. She wouldn't usually, you see. She was drunk.'

'And that makes it all right?'

'I'm scared, Nick. Last night ...'

Nick had a good idea what Rosa alluded to. After exposing her to his hidden world, perhaps her own night under the covers had been fraught with boogeymen. Again, Nick felt a species of guilt. Although ... none of this was *his fault*. Had he ever *wanted* this experience?

Rosa said, 'I didn't say much. Only that we saw people living in the mines, and that's why I was so upset. Homeless people, dangerous types. Mom's too scared to go in there herself, of course. But I think she might call the local police. Anyway, I'm not allowed to go anywhere by myself – even though she's been trying to get me out of the house all week. Nick, you shouldn't go out again alone, either. You won't go back there, will you? Promise me you won't return to that cave?'

I can't do that. Going back there might be the only way of stopping this.

Again, the sentence of the stars came barreling back, somehow brighter and full of more urgency: *Bring another.*

With Rosa's breath ebbing through the

earpiece, Nick remained silent. Finally, when it was clear she had spoken her piece, Nick said, 'Just don't say anything else. I'm in a lot of trouble.'

'Will you talk to me properly, Nick? Tell me what's *really* going on? Are you in any danger? Are you –'

Nick placed the phone back in its cradle.

***

A few hours later, Nick was the cabin's sole occupant when everybody, including Sebastian, disappeared in the family vehicle for Chad's promised exodus into town. Nick's father, feeling magnanimous whenever he could stop into a tavern for a beer, would often let his brood go wandering during these expeditions. Usually this entailed the children partaking of arcade games at Downtown before hot dogs at the Alderwood Mall. Before leaving, neither of Nick's parents had bothered to say goodbye. Not simply a punishment, his exclusion from the trip was also a backhanded message.

You're the black sheep, Ferris Wheel. Get with the Wendy program or get out altogether.

Nick decided to heed the message.

After filling his small backpack with staple edibles, Nick zipped up his jacket and went out into the snow to find Saul.

***

Overnight, Deception Pass had taken a battering, a belated storm over the peninsula lifting entire sections of felled trees and depositing them over the cliff-face Saul Kidman called home. While the sky had cleared by midday, the air was still stagnant, and the clouds smelled of discharge.

In a bleak way, all of this was fitting, Saul thought. Mother Nature, sensing the wonderments underground, had unleashed some splendor of her own.

Absent from yesterday's unveiling, Saul would not be missing for today's encore.

Soon, he would see Nick Wheeler take an even greater step toward his destiny.

And here was the boy now, his slender form weaving through the snow like a lost moor creature, his expression troubled.

***

As he came within earshot of Saul, Nick asked, 'What are you *wearing*? You must be freezing.'

At first, Nick was uncertain the man standing proudly on the slope was his friend at all. Today, for whatever reason, Saul had chosen to wear an immaculate black suit complete with a white bowtie. His cane, usually a brawny companion more in league with a bludgeon, lay clutched against the old man's side like a dapper accessory for an English gent. It was almost comical.

Yet at the same time wasn't.

Rosa told you she saw him wearing a suit.

'Can't a gentleman make his way into the world now and then dressed to the nines?' Saul replied. Seeing Nick's confused look, he laughed. 'I know I must appear a little eccentric, yes. But I like to look my best on important days. And today is a *very* important day.'

'What's special about it? You won't think it is when you hear what I came to tell you.'

'On the contrary,' Saul said. 'I think what you've come here to say will be a defining moment of the morning.'

While Saul usually came equipped with such outlandish rhetoric, the words were peculiar enough for Nick to pause, weighing the rejoinder carefully. Was it possible the old man already knew a portion of what had happened? His behavior, his manner, made this seem likely.

'You were out yesterday,' Saul prompted. 'With that girl.'

'I was,' Nick replied, and though he felt

suddenly uneasy, pressed on. 'She showed me another part of the island, away from here.'

'Through the old mines?'

'How did you know?'

'I have lived here longer than you think, Nick. Longer than you can imagine. I know the arteries of Deception Pass, its secret places, more intimately than anyone alive. You could say I'm like a troll who lives underneath the bridge, always observing the comings and goings of those who pass above me.'

Nick asked, 'Were you spying on us? Following me?'

'Not as you'd understand it, young Nick.'

For a time, Nick said nothing. Simply studied this man whom his parents had cautioned him against. In the time Nick had known him, Saul had never spoken of his home ... Nick's imagination providing details: one of the cabins past the Kuckutali Preserve, he assumed, where retired landowners ran out the clock in the same way Floridians did. And if not there, then where? And how did the old man get around so nimbly, navigating the island's rugged terrain with only the aid of his walking cane?

These were questions that Nick, somewhat hypnotized by the man's genteel aura, had never deigned to ask.

When the silence became uncomfortable, Saul said, 'Your nightmares of the Shadow Men. Have they followed you into the day?'

'Yes,' Nick said, the reply falling from his mouth before he could stop it. 'They're no longer dreams, are they? They never were. Something terrible is happening, and now it's not only happening to *me*. I'm scared that whoever I tell, or whoever I show, will also become *infected*. By the way, that's a word Wendy used to describe me. Infected.'

Close to crying, Nick could feel the helplessness of his affliction threatening to spill out in a torrent, so he decided right then to commence sharing his story. He told of wandering into a tunnel and stepping into a different world; he described strange tenements like a child's building blocks and orange clouds. Finally, he portrayed the Shadows as they moved in their own environment, with backs burnished like an exoskeleton.

At first the dapper-dressed Saul showed little emotion, only nodded in the appropriate places and hastened for Nick to continue. After a time of weighing Nick's words carefully, Saul said, 'Show it to me.'

***

Promise me you won't return to the cave.

They were words uttered only a few hours earlier ... and Nick had held off agreeing. He was returning after all and breaking no promise by doing so. At present, Nick's family would have returned from town, aware of another disappearing act. And Wendy would be sharpening her claws for further reprimands. Strangely, Nick found his capacity to care waning. Justice would no doubt be swift; however, it did not compare to the other threats he faced at night.

And now, paradoxically, the day.

Behind Nick, Saul asked, 'Are you certain this is the way you came in?'

Keeping pace with his younger counterpart, the old man seemed to glide as he walked.

'It's probably not the *exact* way,' Nick replied, relishing the ground they covered because it warmed his bones and delayed the inevitable. 'But near enough. Look, we're here.'

They stood on a precipice looking down, the refuse-filled pond much the same as Nick had seen it the previous afternoon. Banal in the details, really, its outer façade grimy and exposed.

'I'm impressed, Nick,' Saul said, his voice registering exactly that. 'For someone who has seen what you've seen, you showed great courage going in there yesterday.'

It was just to impress a girl, Nick thought, but did not say. The old man's jealousy (and mistrust) of Rosa had been evident since he'd first made mention of her.

Without pausing to consider his actions, Nick bent to the task of scaling the rocky slope, never once taking his eyes off the dark entrance as he did so.

***

Saul had wandered past this particular threshold a few times over the years ... but today, he desired the boy show him, personally. Doing so, Saul sought to observe Nick's reactions and take note of them. While it was true Nick showed signs of apprehension returning, there was also an undeniable curiosity etched on his face. Whether he liked the development or not, Nicholas Wheeler had come to the attention of something miraculous.

And now it fell to Saul Kidman to make introductions.

Only feet from the tunnel, Saul said, 'Wait. We should go in together.'

The boy shrugged, wholly content to keep his gaze fixed on the tunnel.

'Observing strange anomaly in the heavens is one thing,' Saul continued. 'But the best mysteries are not reserved solely for the skies. You see, enigmas often conceal themselves, hiding in secret places.'

'And they only come out at night,' Nick murmured.

Hearing this, Saul's face broke into a stalwart grin – one that (had Nick been looking) he might have shrunk from.

'*Right,*' Saul said, his rictus smile both knowing and somehow maniacal. Proceeding to clap Nick on the back, hard, Saul took a single step into the darkness. 'That's exactly right, young Nick. You're an intuitive boy. One of the many reasons *he* wants to meet you.'

***

Though Saul continued to talk, Nick heard him only peripherally. Having taken his first tentative steps, it was obvious this was going to be a different adventure: no jumping over shallow streams and encountering a second, more puzzling tunnel. This time they were going straight into the heart of the mystery. Ahead, the gloom was already teasing a different firmament.

'Stay close,' he heard Saul whisper. 'You'll want me by your side.'

Exactly what did *that* mean? And what had the old man meant by speaking of a *he*?

Perhaps Saul's been a part of this all along.

Was such a thing possible? Had he been conspiring to lead Nick here today, bereft of the girl whose presence had been enough to extricate them both the first time?

Although Nick's instinct was to pull away, he suddenly felt a hand upon his neck, the fingers caressing, urging him forward with the firm insistence of a parent guiding their child to safety.

***

One moment, a tunnel. The next, a landscape of black glass shouldering edifices Saul had not glimpsed in human lifetimes. Beyond their tips roiled orange clouds so thick and serpentine they were like storms within a gas giant. Lest the scene slow him, Saul pressed forward, one hand still clamped to Nick's shoulder.

'It's as you described,' he said, unable to keep the wonder out of his voice. 'To think ... this has been under our soles the entire time.'

Timidly, Nick asked, 'You knew it was here?'

'I did,' Saul conceded. 'But without you, Nick, I fear it would never have come properly into focus.'

***

When Nick scrutinized the buildings the previous afternoon from a distance, no doors were evident. Yet, here was one now – two rectangles engraved with the insignia of another world.

All morning, Nick had been playing a game of denials. Not only with Saul – but with himself. Feigning ignorance where this journey might end. By not giving a monster its audience, perhaps it would show him indifference when they finally came face-to-face.

Not so. Because the Hat Man has never truly left my side.

That this building was a home to the Hat Man, there could be little doubt. Everywhere, Nick felt his presence. In the energy of the clouds, in the ebb and whorl of the strange insignia. While the entity only played a tourist in Nick's world, peering in through pertinent cracks, this structure was a territory all his own.

Nick felt Saul's hand squeeze his shoulder, and with the sensation, the door widened. First a crack, then an oblong, pushed apart by an invisible force expelling a wake of stagnant air.

Nick had come prepared for theatrics. Because the Hat Man had always been a showman, his grinning visage apropos of the funhouse trade. Yet, here was a demonstration that already subverted those expectations. Looking in, Nick saw two lines of creatures standing like sentries, a corridor between them.

As if from a great distance, Saul's voice floated down. 'They're only statues, Nick. There's no need to be afraid.'

Easier said than done, Nick thought, his whole-body rebelling against the inexorable pull of the corridor. While it seemed true the creatures were indeed statues, these were of a different order: things with zippered faces and anatomies befitting a sphinx.

'They were possibly Shadows once,' Saul said. 'Now, they're about different business.'

Eyeless, the fastened faces provided the suggestion their journey through the corridor was being observed. On Nick's immediate right, a statue's trussed features were in the process of breaking apart. Plaster, patterning downward, exposed a gleam of living tissue.

'Eyes forward,' he heard Saul say. 'Best not look until we reach the end.'

That end came sooner than expected. Once cleared of the statues, another corridor presented itself, this one revealing an object centered in the middle. Some kind of bed, was Nick's first thought. Square, the thing was composed of vines; the bed a nest of twigs and leaves. While smell had only ever been a marginal component of Nick's relationship with the Shadow creatures, looming now was the scent of something altogether inhuman: the blood of tree sap and woodlice rot.

Despite Saul's insistent and ever-present hand, Nick came to a rigid standstill.

'I can't,' he said.

Saul's voice had softened, but it still carried the hallmarks of a staunch tour guide. 'You can, and you will, Nick. This isn't like one of your episodes. I've told you that. This isn't something you can wake from.'

'What *is* this place? Where are we?'

A dark shape chose that moment to emerge beyond the cradle of leaves. Brooding, it was the silhouette of a man wearing a cowboy hat overshadowing a face concealed by pitch-perfect darkness.

A nightmare who had kept him company from early adolescence … it took all the willpower Nick possessed to remain standing.

No longer a cut-out or some half-remembered dream, the Hat Man glided into view like fear itself, masquerading as shadow.

***

Though possessing the power to move, Nick could only stand idle. Saul, also in thrall, appeared waylaid by awe of his own.

Beyond the wide brim of its hat, the elliptical face of the Hat Man spoke.

I've been waiting.

The voice matched the Shadow. Hearing it now, distinctly, there could be little doubt this was the same sandman that nipped and prodded his heels after the sun went down.

My emissary brought you.

So, it was true. Saul had been breaking bread with the enemy all along. And that word ... *emissary*. While Nick had only a cursory grasp of it, Saul's body language told Nick all he needed to know.

This place was a summons.

And he'd been led to the slaughter.

Inching forward, Nick felt waves of energy from the Hat Man like a fetid aroma. And contained within that aroma was every bad experience or thought ... from stubbing his toe in diapers to waking up terrified in a pool of hot sweat from prolonged paralysis.

The moment was brief, only an interlude, but Nick suddenly understood the Shadow creatures *fed* off those things. They took sustenance from human terror in the same way a flea divined blood or a disease attacked its host. The Hat Man, as if sensing this insight, tilted his namesake forward, nodding.

Then he motioned toward the bed of leaves, toward a thing Nick had failed to notice until now.

In the mess of foliage, another hat.

With outstretched fingers, the Hat Man lovingly paraded this prize, a game-show host offering it up as a reward for the taking.

Whatever meaning was implicit, Nick had seen enough.

In normal circumstances, he remained at the mercy of monsters.

But now, he was free to chance another escape.

Though Saul's hand remained attached to his shoulder, Nick shrugged it aside.

Then he turned away from the apparition and began another daring desertion from the land it called home.

7

During his college years, Chad Wheeler was a progressive man. Free to drink copious amounts of beer and take into his bed as many women as his liberal education anointed him. However, the years (and Wendy Fuller), irrevocably changed things. Not solely his alcohol intake, but also his politics. After being on the Democratic ticket for roughly three-quarters of his lifespan, Chad now voted Republican (both in the primaries and the presidential), with the staunch rationale of someone honed by manipulation. Through willful seduction, Wendy transformed Chad Wheeler (from a mild-mannered hippy with dreams of seeing Jimmy Carter to a second term) into a conservative conformist who saw in his three children the same potential for radical renovation. When Wendy Fuller said jump, his unilateral response after three years of marriage was often: how high? When Wendy said his second son should be the recipient of a new kind of discipline, his eventual rejoinder was to fall in line.

Having discovered Nick gone (once again, despite Chad's admonishments he stay put), Wendy retreated, favoring Chad and his children with a brooding quiet. While Chad loved his wife – loved how such a strong-willed woman chose to lavish her attentions on him – he often had trouble recognizing the creature brought into being on each occasion one of his sons flagrantly disregarded the rules.

Oftentimes, the tiger became a lion.

'I want him *gone*, Chad,' Wendy said when she couldn't stand the quiet anymore. 'Gone for good this time. When we return to the city, he can go live with Diana and Peter for a while.'

Diana was Chad's older sister; Peter, his brother in-law. Diana worked as a correctional officer at King County Detention, a prison facility for adults and juveniles. Early in her career, Diana navigated the juvenile system, teasing Chad's children that if they should ever fall out of line, there were plenty of empty beds at juvey waiting for them.

'You're not serious?'

'Of course, I'm *serious*.'

'But Diana is ... unbalanced. You know she had it rough compared –'

'To you and Jim? Yes, I know *all* about that. Exactly why she's perfect. Perhaps, he'll *listen* to your sister. Because God knows, he's stopped listening to either you or me a long time ago.'

So, this was the new kind of discipline she'd been hinting at: shipping Nick off to lands afar. Dump the problem child with someone else, so Wendy could be free of his taint. His *infection*.

'You know he'll never agree to that.'

'It doesn't matter what he wants. He'll have no choice in the matter. Either that or have him stay at one of those halfway houses Dr. Benedict was talking about ... a room where he can be monitored properly.'

'For his dreams?'

'For his dreams. For his *uncouthness*. For making me feel like I'm coming out of my skin in my own damn house.'

Young Bianca, alerted to noise, pushed her bespectacled face through a kitchen archway. Wendy's daughter was smiling ... and Chad knew why. When her mother was angry with Nicholas (or anybody else, for that matter), Wendy would usually dote on her sole child in the aftermath, a subtle game of favorites.

Strange, Chad thought. *Nietzsche was right. In the family unit, competition exists. As much in the human kingdom as it does in the animal one.*

Which recalled his own analogy of Wendy having a tiger's characteristics; Wendy, who was even now, swooping down to rescue her little cub from having to witness anymore turmoil in the pride. Just what would Nietzsche's advice be in all of this, he wondered? Would he have any for Chad Wheeler, a man perpetually caught between a rock and a hard place when it came to his second wife?

'Maybe you're right,' he said, and the look she gave him in return, one full of hope, made him press further. 'When we get back to the city, I'll have a word with Dr. Benedict, see what he thinks of the idea.'

Wendy had taken to stroking Bianca's hair, the motion like an act of grooming. 'I know I was against him going away at the beginning ... but he's not getting any better, is he?'

'No,' Chad replied, already wondering what kind of accolade he would receive for this pandering. Perhaps a blowjob when the kids went to sleep wouldn't be out of the question. Or more: maybe he could even entice Wendy into parting that other, darker hole for him. The one that only seemed to be on offer after they shared a joint.

'He's not getting any better. And to be honest, I think he might embrace the idea of going away for a while. Because let's face it, going by this week's antics, he doesn't want to be a part of this family at all.'

***

In the darkness of his bedroom, Sebastian Wheeler lay wide-awake, watching shadows conjured from the trees outside form patterns on the ceiling. From the room opposite, his parents had ceased their shenanigans – which (judging by the sounds coming through the walls) had involved the kind of sex Sebastian saw in the *Debbie Does Dallas* magazines his friend Brian sometimes swiped from his old man's stash. While Sebastian attempted to block out Wendy's moaning with both fingers and a pillow, his single bed was wedged too close to the wall.

Ferris Wheel, his own bed wedged into the *opposite* corner, had escaped the worst of it.

Which wasn't fair.

Because Chad and Wendy always seemed to go at it like rabbits when Nick was the one acting up. Blowing off steam, Sebastian guessed – his stepmother's rage acting as an aphrodisiac.

Well, it wouldn't last. Tonight, his sleeping brother was put on notice; when the family left Deception Pass at the end of January, Ferris Wheel would be given his walking papers.

Today's disappearing act was the final straw. Were they being too hard on the little prick? Probably.

But seeing Nick walk in the door after supper (his face ashen with terror, his teeth chattering), was enough to cement in Sebastian's mind *something* had to be done. If Ferris Wheel wasn't already a nut job (cuckoo for Cocoa Puffs his friend Brian might have said), then another month in this rural isolation, he soon would be.

Once again, Nick was sent to bed early.

Before getting under the covers himself, Sebastian heard hot sniffles coming from Ferris Wheel's side of the room.

Sebastian recalled the time his father pulled him aside one evening and asked in no uncertain terms if he thought his brother was genuinely sick.

You share a room with him, Seb. You have all your life. What's it like during the worst of his episodes? What do you think he sees?

Nothing, had been his first response. Nothing but phantasms behind closed lids, the kind all dreamers see.

But this wasn't always true.

Occasionally, Sebastian *did* perceive something – a presence in the room like a shady extension of his clothes thrown over a chair. A dark thing that regarded him with the wizened stare of an old hag ... one that saw little boys in the real world as nothing more than food or fodder.

He'd confessed none of this to his father, of course. Because whatever he saw wasn't real, his own imagination working overtime. Listening to tall tales of beings brooding over his bedside could do that to a person. Stories of creatures standing on your stomach and holding you down while you tried to scream but couldn't because you were paralyzed and –

In his bed, Sebastian sat bolt upright.

From the window came a tapping sound.

While gloom played havoc over his brother's side, enough moonlight came through the curtains to reveal a heaped mound of balled-up pillows.

And little else.

His brother's bed was empty.

So, the slippery Ferris Wheel escapes again.

More insistent, the tapping repeated. Sebastian looked out from under his own quilt to see his brother on the other side of the window, his head beanie-clad and his breath frosting the glass.

The tapping sound was from one urgent finger, inviting Sebastian to leave the comfort of his bed and join him in the snow.

***

Until now, Nick was running on instinct. Though he knew what had to be done, carrying it out was an obstacle he felt ill-prepared for. Luring his brother into the night would prove difficult ... but falling short of *dragging* Sebastian out to Saul's slope, little choice existed outside of waking the boy up with false promises.

I've got something to show you, he pleaded through the glass.

'What is it?' his brother asked him on the snowy porch. Standing there, hands fisted against his mouth to stifle the cold, Sebastian looked mad enough to spit. 'You're in deep-enough shit as it is, Ferris Wheel. Why can't this wait until morning?'

While still appearing mad, something about Nick's demeanor must have awoken curiosity in Sebastian, enough for him to brave the night.

'It's my friend,' Nick whispered. 'You know, the old guy? I think you and the others were right about him, after all.'

'What are you *talking* about?'

'He's done something, Sebastian. Something terrible. Something he said he was going to do if I stopped visiting him on the slope. We have to go out there and find him.'

Disbelieving, Sebastian eyed him with the wild stare of the recently awakened. Yet, Nick could also detect another attitude in that look – a thing reserved for the bullies of the world. As if this invitation was an opportunity for Sebastian to participate in a confrontation ... one that would ultimately be forgiven because it was a righteous cause.

'What has he done?' Sebastian asked.

Though Nick was not prepared with any speech, the lies tumbled out easily enough. When Nick spoke to Saul of breaking off their engagements, the old man balked at the idea, becoming someone else in the process – someone he'd surely been from the start. He knew about Rosa Collins, of course, the girl from up the street who was responsible for Nick's change of heart. What would Nick think if Saul decided to pay her a visit one night and snatch her away in the process?

'I don't know for sure if he means to hurt her' Nick said. 'But I need you to come with me and find out.'

***

'I don't understand,' Sebastian was saying. 'If you think he kidnapped the girl, why didn't you just go to Dad or Wendy? Why not call her parents and warn them?'

Navigating Nick's path, the moon's sickle light illuminated serpentine tendrils of fog. Far away, a cormorant released a singular scream, its cry a caveat. While the wind had blown with ferocity earlier, its strength had ebbed to a breeze.

'He was probably only threatening me,' Nick replied, leading the charge without looking back. 'I have to be sure. With you here ... we can threaten *him*. Warn him to stay away from me for good.'

Sebastian said nothing; weighing the notion Nick had chosen him to politick this crisis over anyone else. Part of Sebastian was flattered: Nick giving him the task of playing big brother and defender to his cause. But another part caught scent of a deception ...

Because Nick had *never* charged him with that responsibility.

Not even when their mother was alive.

'What is he, anyway?' Sebastian asked, his intellect provisionally putting aside any misgivings. 'A hobo? A bum? What the hell is he doing outside at this time of the night?'

As though it were a harbinger for more lies, Nick's breath frosted white in the night air. 'He lives underground, in the caves. At least some of the time. During the day, he never leaves his slope.

Tonight will be different, though. He'll be waiting for me.'

'Wait. *What*?'

'Look. We're almost there.'

Above outcroppings of rock wearing coats of frost, the first slivers of sea became visible. First the reflection of moonlight, then the black largesse of Juan de Fuca. Much in the same manner as he did entering the cave with Saul, Nick slowed his pace to a standstill.

While there could be little doubt something immense was about to happen, exactly *what* was as much of a mystery to Nick as the Hat Man's recent show of strength beside his underground bed of leaves.

Sebastian asked, 'What's that?'

'What?'

'*That*,' his brother said, and pointed.

Nick followed Sebastian's finger.

On Saul's slope, an ashen orb of light appeared on an upgrade of earth, a moving circle manipulated by stagehands.

Beyond the light emerged a gauntlet of Shadow creatures.

He sees them! Nick thought with a mixture of euphoria and fear. *Tonight, he's going to see just as Rosa did!*

For a moment, Nick's doubt bloomed, cloying

and full of questions. Was he really going through
with this? Surely not mild-mannered Nicholas
Wheeler; not the boy who shunned violence and
barely spoke above a whisper? Earlier, Saul was the
one ushering a lamb to its slaughter.

Now, it was Nick pulling the reins.

It's too late to back out.

Curious, Sebastian pulled ahead, eyes fixed on
the mystery. As he did so, more light (this of a
darker variety) built and coalesced in the rocks and
trees.

Much as they had in Nick's previous journey
outside his body, the Shadows were behaving in a
manner befitting of beasts.

And becoming fleshier in the process.

All trace of his usual authority receded,
Sebastian asked, 'What's happening? Why did you
take me here?'

Once, during the previous winter, Nick
divulged his fascination with UFOs, regaling
Sebastian with a description of strange things he'd
glimpsed in the sky when standing on this very
slope. His brother, of course, ridiculed the notion ...
then proceeded to make Nick a hat out of cheap
tinfoil filched from the pantry.

Perhaps, Sebastian arrived at this same
conclusion; perhaps, he thought aliens with the lithe
form of lions had landed.

'They're going to send me away,' Nick said, his eyes blurry with the first onset of tears. 'I heard all of it through the wall. Wendy wants me gone, committed somewhere. And she wants to throw away the key. But I won't let that happen. Can't you see I'm not crazy?'

Sebastian could.

Despite Nick's spiel, he failed to turn around or stop moving, completely in thrall with a vista becoming brighter by the moment. Shadows, their crimson eyes illumed as though by headlights, were in the process of being raised from the earth like dead things granted life. Sluggish at first but gaining fresh momentum.

Some, Nick saw, sprouted appendages approximating wings.

One even seemed to carry his own face.

'I'm sorry, Sebastian,' he said. And Nick was ... though he supposed it meant little now. 'I'm tired of trying to run from them. I'm tired of not being *able* to run. You see, they gave me a choice ... someone else or me. And I've *chosen.*'

Was it these words that finally prompted Sebastian's terror? Maybe it was simply the movement of certain Shadows, presently gliding on tenebrous wings, their sights fixed firmly on the boy staggering toward them. Whatever the motivator, Sebastian turned around ... and Nick saw in his expression the panic of something soon to be cornered.

'You *lied* to me.'

Nick did not argue the sentiment. Yes, he had lied. While Saul Kidman was in some way involved with his tormentors, he never threatened Rosa in any capacity.

Nor had the old man made any attempt to block Nick when he'd made his final flight from the Hat Man.

Seeing Nick's admission, Sebastian made a vain attempt to escape. His desire (to remain shielded by the trees) was waylaid before he gained half the distance. In pursuit: a moving phalanx of creatures.

And yes ... one carried his own face.

To the lower portion of the boy's body, they attached themselves, a collision of anatomies. Tripping, Sebastian went airborne temporarily before sprawling headfirst into a pile of snow cushioning the fall.

On the slope, more Shadows became aware of the quarry.

Like predators, they homed; those in flight swooping in a spiral with the agility of eagles.

When Sebastian screamed, Nick fought an overpowering urge to take cover.

No more running, he thought.

Bring another, they had decreed. Yet, there was no certainty the Shadows, seeing the movement of additional prey, would turn their attentions on Nick if he decided to flee.

Because that's the way of predators.

With the wild abandon of dogs, the creatures tore at Sebastian's body. For the moment, they were a group uninterested in feeding on their prey.

Only moving it.

To higher ground.

His tears forgotten; Nick felt a thrill of pleasure at the sight of the Shadows dragging his brother through the snow. At long last, somebody else was at the mercy of this wicked force. *Pain shared is pain halved*, Saul often declared ... and here was evidence: Shadow creatures transporting the meat of his brother toward the edge of a cliff as though he'd been singled out from a herd.

The edge.

Looming large and lit by a strange light, Saul's slope was now revealed like the stark outline of pointed piranha teeth, jigsaw corners giving leeway where the boy would end up. As if sensing this imminence, Sebastian loosed yet another agonizing howl, this time peppering his cries with Nick's name.

You'll never call me Ferris Wheel again. Not you ... not anybody else. Tonight, I retire that name for good.

And this, Nick realized, was the purpose of any sacrifice. By giving Sebastian to the Shadows, he was sloughing off his adolescence and everything that came with it: his self-inflicted isolation; his relationship with entities that preyed upon the human mind.

Saul Kidman might even call this an act of bravery.

Saul.

And here was the enigma, returned to his slope. His cane held crosswise, Saul beamed down at Nick and smiled. Had the old man been there all along? Yes, Nick thought, perhaps he had. Just like the Hat Man, Saul Kidman could pick and choose when to step out of the shadows. Eager to be of service to the night, Saul beckoned the creatures forward with their prize.

In a melee of twisting limbs, they reached the summit.

And disappeared over the edge.

From *Skagit Breaking Community News*:
December 15, 1984

ACCIDENTAL DECEPTION PASS FALL KILLS LOCAL BOY.

A 15-year-old boy has died at Deception Pass in what appears to be an accidental fall near Fidalgo Island, sometime between Sunday evening and Monday morning.

Arlington resident, Sebastian Wheeler fell from a cliff located north of Deception Pass Bridge, said Park Ranger Nick Garnett.

Garnett said he started looking for Sebastian when his family called Monday morning after noticing his coat and glasses lying near the edge of the cliff. Garnett said he hiked down a scramble route to the rocks below and discovered Sebastian's body, who fell approximately 80 feet to the rocks. Talus slope, which is basically loose rocks that gather at the base of a cliff, accounted for the remaining 50 feet down to the water.

While Deception Pass Bridge has been the site of numerous suicides in recent years, suicide doesn't seem to be the cause of Sunday night's death.

'It appears to be an accident,' said Clayton Williams, chief criminal deputy for the Skagit County Sheriff's Office. He stressed, however, that the case was still under investigation.

After Garnett discovered the boy's body, local park rangers and firefighters from North Whidbey Fire and Rescue transported Sebastian's body to the boat landing at Cornet Bay where the Skagit County Coroner's Office took custody of the body.

PART THREE

Hidden City

1

There were no winged cherubs to escort Nick back into the land of the living, nor tunnel of light. Upon first opening his eyes, it was Hayley's voice acting as a smelling salt; her whispers urging her father to join her in a room redolent of antiseptics and flowers gone to seed.

At first the voice was unfamiliar ... as foreign and elusive as his own name. Then the syllables were joined by black lipstick, blue eyeshadow, and cat's-eye prescription glasses.

'Chicken,' Nick managed, speaking around lips so fallow it was like pressing his tongue against sandpaper.

His private nickname for Hayley, used only

sparingly since she'd begun applying the makeup, was all the fuel needed to ignite the first wave of tears ... tears of relief and gratitude that would flow into the days and weeks as Nick began his slow process of recovery.

His fall from inside the Canlis building had broken no bones; however, the impact and subsequent head trauma was enough for doctors to induce a temporary barb-coma – a week in which they had (often privately) wondered if the man who took macabre pictures for a living would survive to tell the tale.

***

'A barbiturate coma?' Nick asked. 'That sounds a lot more fun than it actually is.'

'Carefully administered, barbiturates reduce the metabolic rate of brain tissue, and hence, intracranial pressure. With the swelling relieved, the pressure decreases; some, if not all, potential brain damage can be averted.'

'I've averted all brain damage?'

Dr. Jenkins was a mild-mannered man in his forties surrounded by two fawning interns who reminded Nick of baby ducklings following their mother.

Smiling, Jenkins replied, 'From everything

you've exhibited so far since awakening – your speech patterns, your gait, your memory – this appears to be the case. If you continue to improve like this, I have little doubt you'll make a full recovery.'

In his hospital bed, Nick shifted to accommodate a still-aching back. 'My memory ... I don't *remember* falling. I can recall some things – like Andrea being there. But everything else is a blank.'

One of the interns looked up and favored Nick with a strange look he couldn't interpret.

'Dissociative amnesia, mild in your case, is perfectly normal after blunt cranial trauma. Certain information can be blocked out in relation to the upsetting event. In time, I imagine most of the details will return.' Jenkins tipped Nick a small nod. 'That is, if you *want* to remember. Personally, I don't think you should be in any rush to. It wasn't pretty. But you're luckier than some – luckier than most. It was a fall where any number of things could have happened but didn't. Your working partner, colleague, what was her name?'

'Andrea.'

'Yes. The experience wasn't pleasant for her, either. Have you had an opportunity to call her?'

'Not yet,' Nick admitted. 'But I'll get on it soon.'

'I think you should. Tell her how you're feeling. That you're basically okay. She was very upset the night you came in.'

Nick could imagine. While Andrea was a true professional when it came to their craft – the illusion of it all – anything that smacked of real-life calamity often had a way of bruising her.

'She's a true artist,' Nick said. 'Hence, a sensitive soul. I'll talk to her first thing tomorrow.'

To this, there was concrete silence. The professionals, no doubt, were brooding on his and Andrea's chosen vocation. Had Jenkins taken the time to Google Nick's work history in between doing his rounds? Almost certainly. And what he'd discovered obviously went against the grain of what it meant to be a practitioner of the healing arts.

Nicholas Wheeler, a suicide photographer, *also* dabbled in death. But their ideologies for doing so were as far removed from each other as the principles between angels and demons.

'Do you have any questions?' Jenkins wanted to know.

'Just the million dollar one,' said Nick. 'How long before I can go home?'

***

As things turned out, much sooner than

anybody (including Nick's cadre of doctors) could have predicted. While Nick shuffled with a limp for a few days after leaving his bed, he soon developed the agility to shower without the aid of a walker or even his wife's shoulder. His mental faculties, often blurred with a menagerie of painkiller opioids, swiftly clarified after his dosage was whittled down to a singular OxyContin after dinner.

'I'm proud of you,' Heidi said between feeding Nick spoonfuls of tomato soup. Though he could perform the task himself, Heidi took a simple pleasure in doting. 'The Nick I married would have taken an Oxy before breakfast then asked for another after. Who is this stranger before me?'

Someone who remembers his childhood too clearly, Nick thought. *The doctors say dissociative amnesia comes after head trauma. But nobody tells you reliving your past is also a side effect.*

'What's wrong?' Heidi asked, noticing his sudden, downcast mood. 'What did I say?'

'There were ... dreams while I was under. Though not the type you're thinking of.'

Placing his spoon back into the plastic bowl, Heidi scooted closer to the serving tray. Leaning forward, she spoke in a conspiratorial whisper. 'Hayley's been bugging me to ask you day and night. Even my Mom said something, to be honest. They want to know –'

'If I had some kind of near-death experience? Did my boogeymen decide to pay me a visit while you guys were waiting for me to wake up?'

'Something like that,' Heidi admitted. Though she smiled, there was little humor in her next words. 'I told Hayley I didn't really want to know. Nick ... there were moments after you fell, terrible ones when they had trouble containing the swelling. We thought – *I* thought – you weren't going to make it.'

An unconscious gesture, Nick reached under the tray and found his wife's hand. He said, 'You were right. I shouldn't have gone to work that morning. I should've listened to you and stayed home.'

Despite the somber turn, Heidi laughed. 'Now, I *know* this isn't the real Nick talking. What happened? Did the fall knock some sense into you?'

For a moment, all Nick could picture was the old man he'd given little thought to for almost three decades: Saul Kidman. He thought of Saul standing on his slope, grinning down at Nick with the kind of leer that would shame the Devil. Though Nick had made the decision days ago regarding his future, it was Saul's visage which made his next choice of words feel like proper ones.

'It's over, Heidi. It should have been over *years* ago. The pictures I take ... it's all a disgusting illusion that's about as hollow as an evangelist.

145

What happened to me in Deception Pass – there's *a lot* I haven't told you. About what really happened to my brother, Sebastian. I never told you that it was my fault, did I? Or that my pictures are just a reflection of the self-hate I feel *because* it was all my fault?'

'You've told me *everything*, Nick.'

'No, I haven't. Not really. I don't think I've brushed the surface. My dad still blames me for Sebastian's death, did you know that? Because he knows, you see. He knows I lured Sebastian out to Saul's slope that night.'

'You're not making any sense. Your brother *fell*. It was an accident. Just like the one that put you in here.'

This, coming from Heidi's scant knowledge, surprised him. Why hadn't he been able to see the synchronicity at work? Sebastian was dragged ... and then flung from a great height by a pride of roving demons.

Perhaps you were, too.

Nick's recollection of events prior to losing his balance was haphazard. He remembered the scaffolding; he remembered Andrea as a pinprick of a person. After that, his memory glossed over certain pictures and scenes.

Pictures.

'What happened to my camera?' he asked

abruptly, putting forth a question he should have from the beginning.

As if knowing this moment would arrive, yet loathe to giving it an audience, Heidi gestured toward the bedside drawers where Nick's personal belongings had been sequestered.

'It's in there with the rest of your stuff.'

'It survived?'

'In one piece.'

***

Discharged that night, Heidi drove them home; Nick wedged in the passenger seat of her Subaru with a pair of forearm crutches strafed between his legs. His progressive resurgence back to optimal health – where every hour saw improvements in his overall movement – had been declared a minor miracle by his team of specialists.

'Jenkins said the business of life and death should possess a mystical quality,' Heidi told him. 'He seems to think your recovery has some kind of numinous element attached.'

'Numinous? Where did you hear that word? Did Hayley teach it to you?'

She slapped his thigh. 'Such wit. I still *read*, you know. By the way, she's beside herself about you coming home. If her tutor is feeling generous, he'll give her an early release, and she'll make it home before we do.'

'Bass lesson?'

'Six string. She switched about a month ago. You don't remember?'

'Vaguely. Though, I'm not surprised. Everyone drops the bass eventually. Remember that *Simpson's* episode when Homer –'

'Goes to rock 'n' roll camp?' Heidi grinned. 'Yeah, I remember. Tom Petty was the one handing out guitars before Homer climbs over him to –'

'Get an electric,' Nick finished, laughing 'And what did Mick Jagger say?'

'Cheer up, Homer. It's *only* rock 'n' roll camp.'

'I know, but I *like* it.'

Mild guffaws became full-throated laughter. Bent forward to better see the road through her giggles, Heidi said, 'I've *missed* you, Nick. Can you please do me a favor? Don't try to die again anytime soon.'

'What? Are you saying our daughter isn't providing the laughs at home as of late?' Nick asked, the question a repartee given Hayley's goth-centric worldview.

'She hasn't been herself,' Heidi admitted. 'But then, neither have I. Please don't take this the wrong way, but there have been times during our marriage when I thought having a break from you would be a good thing. Not having to share your nightmares for a while. Just ... the bliss of uninterrupted sleep, you know?' Heidi paused, seemed to weigh all that followed carefully. 'But *not* having you next to me has been worse, somehow. Your side of the bed – it's like this void. A kind of weird vacancy that someone or something else has become aware of.'

Stranger than usual words, Nick thought. He knew – with the unique understanding of couple's parlance – what Heidi was alluding to. Someone or *something* else wasn't another person or potential suitor; she was giving lip-service to Nick's midnight persecutors. Those beings, who were in all probability, aware of his absence from home and decried a condition where they were deprived holding their court of nightmare.

'You don't have to worry,' he said, staring out at the passing houses, knowing in his heart she had many reasons to worry. 'I don't plan on dying today or tomorrow. Ferris wheels are built to last.'

Heidi glanced at him. For a few seconds, she simply stared, wondering why Nick chose to resurrect a childhood nickname.

It's the first time I've said it in years.

Ten minutes later, they were pulling into Nick's driveway. On the grass, a smiling and relieved Hayley Wheeler stood, ready to greet them.

2

Over the years taking photographs – first for fun, then for profit – Nick dreamt of owning the ultimate darkroom. A begrimed space of chemical baths with the ambiance of a torture chamber. Producing art (he'd always extolled) should never be a comforting experience. Instead, it should be fashioned in an incubator every bit as rough and tumble as the raw, biological workings of a uterus.

While his studio *almost* fit this criterion, it had (since the advent of digital photography) evolved into more of a storage space than a genuine darkroom. The once-brimming baths were now filled with the detritus of used negatives. The room's centerpiece, a giant enlarger, had also fallen into disrepair.

Stepping into the darkroom, Nick switched on a bank of fluorescents in his wake.

Off-limits to both Hayley and Heidi, Nick still used his studio to develop film on the rare occasion he used an old camera.

His digital pictures were printed, then hung.

There were dozens of them plastered to every available wall space, hanging like laundry on makeshift hangers.

Dirty laundry ...

Dirty because the pictures ran a gamut of the gruesome. There were shooting deaths and highway deaths; there were guillotines and homemade gallows.

Comprising the bulk were suicides arranged like a cabinet of curiosities, inviting any casual observer to invariably draw the conclusion his darkroom was the domicile of a madman or masochist.

Every picture was a cunning illusion, the victims either mannequins or models.

Standing only feet away, Nick studied his collection as though seeing it under the gauze of new eyes.

How had he functioned thinking any of this was normal?

How had his wife?

And just what gave him the right to pedal death as though it were a commodity?

Slowly, Nick came to the closest photo. This one depicted the murder and suicide of a mother and her children. After skewering two boys to a kitchen table with an assortment of utensils, an older sibling had been impaled with a machete. This fictitious mother, in the aftermath of murdering her fictitious children, proceeded to blow half her face off with a large handgun. Her body, along with her ejected life-stuff, lay cooling on top of the counter like an animal arranged as an offering.

Demand for the tableau came from a man named Gerard Roberts, a fortyish father of three who surreptitiously despised his family unit. With Nick's help, he concocted a fantasy detailing their ultimate demise.

Andrea provided a mold for the mannequin. This, coupled with real photos of Gerard's wife, gave Nick enough leeway to create a doppelganger. On the mannequin's upper arms were scabbed over scratches, a detail Gerard specifically requested. The scratches were a pragmatic form of realism, he explained, evidence one of the children had briefly fought back against its mother. Gerard, having the wherewithal to obtain his money's worth, even appealed for a suicide note.

Nick, writing the letter himself, placed it on the

woman's gore-streaked diaphragm.

I'm as bad as Gerard for doing this.

It wasn't the first time his conscience cried foul. Ethical objections were somewhat part and parcel of the trade. Yet this time, there was no dissenting voice raised in opposition. No rejoinders that Nick Wheeler was simply a *businessman* who saw artistic merit in this wanton besmirching of human life.

You can try telling yourself free-market capitalism is the real demon if you want. It doesn't change the fact this profession is a morally bankrupt endeavor.

Not just morally bereft: a stain on his psyche, overall.

For most of his remembered life, Nick dealt with exterior demons. Creatures who, after the death of his sibling, only departed temporarily.

So, why did Nick feel the need to subject himself to further horrors, piling one atop the other during the daylight hours until no disparity existed with the night?

Because you've always thought of this art as therapy.

Yes, he had. But ...

'It's the *opposite* of therapy,' Nick said aloud. The sound – amplified in the enclosed space – caused him to retreat a step.

Doing so, his eyes alighted on a workbench.

And the digital camera posited there by Heidi the previous night.

The camera used in the Canlis shoot.

***

Too frightened to inspect the camera at his hospital bedside, Nick did so now, holding it up to the fluorescent light as though evidence of damage would be obvious. As Heidi had declared back in hospital, no visible damage existed.

Nick thumbed the ON switch.

Taken from inside the Canlis building, the images emerged. Practice shots at first, Nick's eye hovering over tables covered with mildew and rodent droppings. Crouched over bags of makeup, her back to the camera, was one of Andrea. Subsequent pictures revealed a dead woman lying on the cement, her face a suppurating mask.

Rope-burns crisscrossed a bloated neck.

Cassandra.

Like a picture clearing in a vat of water, Nick's memory began to reassert itself.

Acquired by Andrea, Cassandra would enact a standard hanging, the backdrop an abandoned restaurant. Nick, sensing an opportunity, had scaled a girder of maintenance platforms, there to frame his subject in a series of aerial shots.

Here were the results: a victim suffering rigor-mortis, her tongue protruding from putrescent lips.

Cassandra's eyes, feigning the illusion of death, abruptly bulged with life.

Sensing something.

Entering from the right, a Shadow materialized. First, a proboscis sampling the counterfeit corpse, then a torso. With every picture, more Shadows entered the frame.

By the time they turned their attentions upward, six creatures stood in the shot.

Seeing them bleed into reality (tangible evidence in three dimensions) quickened Nick's heart rate and breath.

In addition to the snouts were the suggestion of eyes, windows both demonic and malign.

Finally, here they were.

Entities not viewed under the pall of sleep paralysis or experienced through a myopic lens of the past.

Besides Heidi, the only other individual privy to his childhood in Deception Pass was his general practitioner, Helen Sinclair, who counseled him that at no time had these creatures breached the real world. That was a child's recollection, superimposed with wild embellishment. Yes, Nicholas Wheeler was at the mercy of a deadening condition, but the apparitions glimpsed in these episodes were brought about by a hyper-vigilant state created by the midbrain.

Shadow Men were nothing more than endogenous stimuli to a perceived threat.

Then what are these?

Three stared directly into the maw of Nick's camera, smudged jaw lines like a hyena's leer.

'Nick?'

From the doorway came the sound of Heidi's voice.

'Jesus,' he muttered, and let out a shaky, pent-up breath. 'You scared me.'

Heidi kept one foot on the first riser of a small staircase. Her head – wrapped in a bath-towel – was only partially visible.

'I'm not surprised,' she said. 'Not the first time it's happened, and probably won't be the last. Are you done here for the night? Come to bed. I switched on your side of the electric.'

'Has Hayley turned in?'

'Just about.'

'I'll be up in two minutes,' he said, and meant it. But first ...

'Heidi? You didn't bother looking, did you?'

'At what?'

'The camera. The one that survived?'

'Of course not. You know I don't have the

stomach for your work anymore.'

<u>3</u>

Sheathed in black ice, the road to Deception Pass is sometimes transparent. With every turn, Nick's reflection becomes visible, a barreling wraith brandishing two poles. On the horizon, like a partially glimpsed leviathan, Mount Rainier pokes its glaciated head above a seething band of cloud.

No cars litter this highway.

There is only snow, ice, and the looming threat Nick could topple over at any moment and paralyze his spine.

He thinks: Can that happen in a dream?

Another hairpin looms; this one saddled with a roundabout, and before Nick can break, he's already flying over it, his skis airborne before landing smoothly on the other side.

Surely, you couldn't become paralyzed in a dream?

With the thought comes increased speed, and Nick is suddenly whooshing past dozens of cabins, their front façades dotting the landscape like spirit houses.

Logic, not always prevalent in dreams, insists this MUST be a dream ...

Because Nick Wheeler, despite spending large parts of his childhood on the outskirts of a state park, has never learned how to properly ski.

Nevertheless, he slaloms the unploughed highway with a lackadaisical, almost professional grace. Below, Nick's ever-present reflection is like some bizarre shadow twin.

Shadows.

Shadows are known to haunt Deception Pass.

Of course, this had been the destination all along: Nick Wheeler is returning home to a place where strange slopes revealed secret entrances and strange men prowled pathways. Would the family's cabin still be there? Almost certainly. Things seldom changed in Deception Pass ...

With the kind of narrative shift typical of dreams, he's suddenly skiing on a familiar road. In the distance, Chad Wheeler's old property is a petite smudge hugging the horizon.

On the road's shoulder stands a silhouette: that of a young girl. Rosa Collins, he realizes. Rosa, who has not aged a day with the passage of time. Sporting a thick winter hood, Rosa brandishes a cardboard sign like a hitchhiker. Edging closer with every ski stroke, Nick can make out four words emblazoned on the sign in red paint:

THE HAT MAN COMETH.

Of course, he does.
What kind of reunion would it be without a rumor that Nick's boyhood boogeyman was going to be among the returning cast members? Although the head honcho had been scarce for years, Nick was perpetually aware of his presence like the fleeting glimpse of stagehands behind a curtain. Yes, architects and engineers sometimes disappeared for long durations, but they were never TRULY gone. They –
Rosa slid past, and Nick saw the face inside her hood was a dead one. Within a purple crescent of pale rot, Rosa's vacant eyes followed his passage like a zombie.
A message? Nick wondered. Some kind of warning? Had Rosa Collins perished since his leaving, possibly succumbing to an accident of her own?

He was streaming near the cabin. Had he thought it occupied before? Perhaps it had been, once. Now, abandonment reigned: its outer façade bleached white by the elements; the red-tiled roof gray with decay. Thinking this was a pitstop, if not his outright destination, Nick attempted to turn.

But only met resistance.

His old home wasn't the endgame, after all.

Soon it was gone, and Nick was navigating a path he hadn't turned his thoughts to since leaving college and taking up residence in the suburbs of Seattle.

How did I forget about this path?

Though a better question would be: Why had he assumed the ultimate objective here would be anything other *than where it led?*

Saul's slope, the grass portion completely covered in snow; its ridgeline a jagged formation like the spine of a sleeping dragon. Familiar boulders crowded a territory of land infested with gossamer Shadows.

Alerted to Nick's presence, they began to move, jostling like a river of rats in thrall to the suited figure who brooded above them.

'Welcome back, Nick!' Saul bellowed from his mound. Unlike the hill itself – which showed visible erosion – Saul hadn't aged a day. 'What do you think of my soldiers? They're new and improved,

Nick! New and improved!'

He's talking about the Shadows, Nick thought. Somewhere in the journey, he'd lost both skis – more dream logic.

'That's right!' Saul yelled, as if reading the thought. 'In your day, they were fledgling children, nursing at the tits of a world only beginning to go bad. But look at them now! See how they've grown!'

Nick looked – and Saul was right. The Shadows, somewhat ephemeral things in the world of 1984, had grown disproportionally in shape and size. Having compared them with dogs and tigers in the past, it was safe to assume these were neither.

On Nick's left moved a creature more in league with a dinosaur, its back a plumage of plates. Its head – inverted like a shark – contained glistering eyes that mirrored back the world like puddles of black oil.

Beyond the dinosaur moved a shape with a reptile's swagger. Its only claim to a cranium: an open sheath of gut it wore like a mask. Close to Saul's feet scampered a smudge whose mammalian anatomy hinted at a rodent, its outline of whiskers frisking the air.

Similar beasts were everywhere; a fawning parade who loped, stalked, and sometimes flew on the winds of a world under a perpetual noon.

'And the sun is no longer their enemy!' Saul

shouted, again, seeming to read his thoughts. 'Nick, you need to come home. Come home and see the wonders they're setting in motion.'

There it was: an admission this vision was a kind of calling. Except Nick wasn't being summoned back to a gothic estate called Manderley. No, a small island was beckoning; an archipelago whose breeze contained the clement scent of another dimension bursting at the seams to be born.

'You killed my brother,' Nick said, his first words since stepping into the dream.

'But we didn't,' Saul replied. 'Come home, Nick. Or should I call you Ferris Wheel? Your brother is a lot closer than you think.'

At this, the parade of creatures stirred, then began to part before Saul like a proverbial sea.

Here comes the final piece of the puzzle, Nick thought. Soon, a sinister man is going to lurch through the throng. Perhaps, for the occasion, he would be wearing a graduation hat. Like his minions, he would be new and improved, imploring his old subject to return to Deception Pass.

Except it wasn't the Hat Man.

Another Shadow, this one twice as large as its companions, emerged with all the grace of a walrus. At first, Nick thought the creature equipped with natural wings ... but a closer inspection revealed its own lungs and viscera served as flying extensions, a blood eagle born.

Its head, like the giant skull of a fetus, contained Sebastian Wheeler's features.

'You see!' Saul Kidman sang. 'Sebastian didn't die. He became something more!'

Over spittle-slicked tusks, the Sebastian-thing gibbered and laughed.

***

Snapping awake, Nick opened his eyes in the mundane environment of his bedroom. Beside him, Heidi moaned. Coming up from her own sleeping position, she regarded him with questioning and unfocused eyes.

'Just a dream,' he said. 'Not an episode.'

'You're certain? Look at yourself.'

The sheet clinging in places, Nick's arms and chest were slicked with sweat.

'I *did* dream them. But it was away from here.'

Swinging herself out of bed, Heidi asked, 'Where?'

'Deception Pass. What time is it?'

Consulting her phone, Heidi stretched and groaned. 'Morning. I have to get Heidi to a hair appointment. By the way, you're seeing Helen this afternoon.'

'What?'

'I made an appointment for today. Don't fight me on this, either. She called while you were in the hospital. Jenkins emailed her a discharge summary.'

'The gory details,' Nick muttered.

'What?'

'Nothing. I'll be there.'

***

Later, Nick reflected on the brief exchange, wondering how his wife would have reacted if posed the question Nick had been considering asking since awakening.

Heidi – I want to return to Deception Pass. In fact, I think I need to. What do you think of that?

Twelve years of marriage gave him the answer. At first Heidi would ridicule the notion, then – after some prolonged back and forth – potentially accede.

Though not without bringing forth a host of observations related to his personal habits, which included driving past (and occasionally pulling up to) old homes they had rented in the years before Hayley was born.

You visit them trying to glean something – I don't know what. Measuring what you have now compared to what you had then, I suppose. A kind of stock take. But nothing can be gleaned from the past, Nick. Only ghosts. And what do ghosts do?

They haunt.

Of course, Heidi had known from the beginning that Nick was a haunted man. Predisposed to brooding and introspection. Traits psychologists often associated with the symptoms of clinical depression. It was, when you got right down to it, the way of all men. And marriage (in theory) was supposed to cure the ailment; scourge clean the slate of dogmas inflicting the husbands and sons of the world. In Nick's case, his marriage *had* worked to an extent. Because a buried optimist emerged in the aftermath.

But matrimony (or anything of its ilk, like having a child for instance) only ever worked as a temporary gauze to the invisible burdens that plagued his sex.

I'm not going back to relive the past; Nick would explain to this hypothetical Heidi. *Only to close the door on it.*

But what is going back really about, Nick? Your sleep paralysis or your brother? If it's the latter and the guilt you feel over how he died, then I won't stop you from going anywhere.

After finally consenting, Heidi would insist they travel together – all of them – as a family.

Which cannot happen.

No, it couldn't. Because in addition to being bound by a covenant to protect them, Nick had no inkling as to the kind of mysteries lying in wait. It was true he recalled a great deal while comatose, but how many of those memories were occluded by a biased mind? Last night's dream of Saul's slope, though vivid, could potentially be more phantasmagorical foolery from a brain already hotwired for stunning illusions.

And that's where my father and stepmother come in. I need to hear their versions – another step to uncovering the mystery.

Thinking of talking to Wendy Fuller now – Wendy in her present incarnation as the matriarchal caregiver to a crude, old man with the onset of dementia – abolished any thought of having Heidi or Hayley in tow.

Years ago, he vowed they would never be in the same room together.

So, decided his return to Deception Pass would be a solo affair, Nick pulled out his personal laptop.

***

Finding suitable accommodation on Whidbey Island in November (his first task) was waylaid by seeing a browser history that read like a greatest hits catalogue pertaining to sleep paralysis. Normally steadfast at clearing his Internet activity, Nick had recently failed to do so. Derelict in deletion, he had *also* forgotten to minimize last night's searches. While some articles were familiar (*Sleep Demons In The Age of Science* read one), there were at least two that weren't.

One wasn't an article at all.

More like a brochure.

Showcasing a large cabin and its present availability to any would-be prospector.

Hayley must have been goofing around on this laptop last night. I wasn't the one looking at this.

Which was absurd. It was a strict edict in the Wheeler household to *never* use each other's laptops. Not for anything. The same rule applied to phones. For gaming, Nick had purchased a cheap communal computer that lived out its days on a small desk beside the kitchen table.

So, who was looking at the cabin where I grew up?

No question, this was it – the same land where Nick once helped to hollow out a racing track. Owned by Chad Wheeler and his wife until the late Eighties, the cabin was presently being leased as a vacation rental.

Your typical Airbnb with photos and guest reviews.

During the Nineties, or Noughties, an additional floor had been constructed. Its pointed roof, pronounced, gravitated toward a steeple.

Coupled with overarching bay windows, the cabin had the distinct flavor of a tree house.

Which explained the page's heading: *Deception Tree House.*

Since Hayley entered the world, Nick's swearing had dried up considerably ... yet he cursed now, the word reverberating back through the kitchen and hallway.

Deception Tree House was available to rent for $189.00 a night.

Below digital photographs of the house sat a user profile with the grinning visage of a white-haired man. Should you want to escape to this romantic Deception Pass getaway, *he* was the man you contacted.

Without thinking, Nick clicked on the icon.

***

In the suburb of Bellevue, Helen Shekel's practice was nestled between a real estate office and a small cafe. With a caseload of deliberately undersized patients, Helen's waiting room was also small, the plastered posters few and subtle. While some of the usual suspects were in evidence – *JOIN THE FIGHT, TAKE UP YOUR BREAST SCREENING INVITE* read the one above Nick's head –there were also a couple reflective of Helen's casual sense of humor. Between a cartoon doctor and patient, the punch line read *YOUR X-RAY SHOWED A BROKEN RIB, SO WE FIXED IT WITH PHOTOSHOP.*

With some initial reservation, Helen acquiesced to see Nick fourteen years ago. The reluctance sprung from Nick's personal circumstances: Helen Shekel was not a clinical psychologist, nor did she officially specialize in sleep disorders. However, her referral came from a mutual friend, Stacey ... someone who *also* flirted with midnight apparitions.

She's the only doctor who's ever taken me seriously, Stacey passed on before his first appointment. *She'll see you but don't come right out with your condition. Ease her into it.*

Nick had done so – only mentioning *Shadow Men* once an initial rapport was established. Then, Helen divulged a clinical name for Nick's abnormalities: Parasomnia. Of which there were essentially two types: Predormital (when falling asleep) and Postdormital (when waking up).

While hearing Helen's information came as a relief, Nick felt an even greater sense of liberation knowing he was in the company of someone who took the affliction seriously. Too often (when first diagnosed during the early Eighties, for instance), Nick's practitioners tended to shrug off the experience entirely, reasoning the paralysis aspect to be a psychosomatic burden.

And therefore, not a serious medical risk.

In the aftermath of their initial discussions, Helen developed a plan of attack, including (but not limited to) antidepressant medication and ongoing cognitive behavioral therapy. Ultimately, this psychoanalysis led to Nick opening up about his winters in Deception Pass.

'Mr. Wheeler?

Nick looked up at the smiling brunette behind the counter, startled from waiting room reverie. Helen's help was only a few years older than Hayley (give or take), yet wore the role of receptionist like a pro.

'Helen will see you now.'

***

'For someone who has just had a small brush with death, I feel fantastic.'

Alternating her attention between a computer monitor and Nick, Helen replied, 'You look it, too. Almost all the bruising has vanished. Reading your accident summary, I was almost afraid Rip Van Winkle would come ambling through my door.'

Today, in keeping with her informal character, Helen wore a pale-blue boxy top and jeans. Arrayed on her desk blotter (even more reflective of the doctor's persona), a *Buffy the Vampire Slayer* figurine stood brandishing a stake.

'Jenkins sent me away with a clean bill of health. Ostensibly, I'm here to get another prescription of Paroxetine. But I could also use some advice.'

After fourteen years of spilling his guts to Helen – in one instance literally after a bout of intestinal flu – Nick would often take a personal tact.

'I've left my profession. And before you furrow your brow, you know I've been dallying with the idea for years. This ... recent accident just gave me the impetus.'

No surprise from the doctor.

'For the time being, we'll be okay. At least until early next year. And that gives me some time to travel, a sabbatical, perhaps. I'm thinking about returning to the coast.'

Cue the first lie, Nick thought. *I hit the reserve button for Deception Tree House before I could blink.*

Adroit at reading his body language if not his mind, Helen asked, 'Where you grew up? You're thinking about going back to Whidbey Island?'

'What do you think?'

'That depends. I remember you floating the idea some time ago ... in addition to walking away from photography. Back then, the ambition seemed to be nothing more than a brief holiday.'

'Where my family would tag along?'

'Precisely. You talked about showing Heidi some of your local haunts. Kayaking to one of the remote places instead of taking the ferry. But you're not talking about that kind of adventure, are you?'

'No.'

Nick proceeded to outline his intentions, which included organizing some sort of permanent memorial at the slope where Sebastian fell ... something his stepmother had expressly forbidden in the aftermath. Her reasons for doing this (both perplexing and infuriating) stemmed around the belief any permanent plaque would cause division in the family. At the time, Nick was adult enough to see a fostered lie: Wendy didn't want any enduring fixture because it gave Sebastian (who wasn't really *her* child) more attention than he was deserving of.

Helen said, 'Only a few minutes ago, you used the words *brush with death*. Do you feel physically capable of travelling?'

It could be just what the doctor ordered, Nick thought to reply, then settled for a perfunctory *sure*. What Helen said next, however, illumined the question had been nothing more than simple rote rhetoric.

'Heidi and I spoke briefly while you were in

your coma. Do you remember promising her you'd come and see me just before the accident? It was one of the last things you spoke about before leaving that morning. She told me your sleep paralysis had returned, and your episodes were increasing in frequency and becoming darker in context. She mentioned there might be levels of physicality involved?'

Triggered by the words, Nick felt the phantom recall of physical pain first spreading through his abdomen, then conjoining with his genitals.

How did I forget the Shadow claw scything my balls? That thing was like the Hat Man's personal pitchfork ...

Unable to hide his discomfort, Nick said, 'I guess you could say that.'

'You want to talk about it?'

Nick did. He wanted to talk about everything ... not just the physical pain. He wanted to talk about how – in the cold months after Sebastian's death – the Shadows had first honored their agreement, retreating to their hidden city of black glass. And how they had surely taken his brother's soul with them. At least, this had been Nick's overriding thought: that a toll had been paid. In lieu of Nick's, Sebastian Wheeler's essence was now the plaything of demons.

Only, the reprieve proved temporary.

Six months later, Nick was once again becoming rigid and inflexible after falling asleep. By the time the holidays commenced in the fall, the beings returned en masse.

Rather than confess any of this, Nick said, 'I've been reading it's not unusual. That a person experiencing paralysis can undergo brief levels of physical pain. Sufferers online share combat methods, ways to handle it.'

'You've joined a support group?'

'Sort of. Although we don't physically get together. Mostly, it's just knowing you're not alone.'

'That sounds beneficial.'

Here comes another lie ...

'The pain involved is like anything in dreams – just the body's natural reaction to stimuli. It might sometimes hurt, but you're never going to wake up with scars or bleeding.'

Helen sat silent, regarding her computer notes as though tasked with something unpleasant. 'If you want a permission slip from me to do this trip, then you have it. I actually think revisiting your place of trauma is long overdue. However, I also think you've come seeking outside authorization because other parties might not be so open to the idea.'

She sees everything.

'If the thought of broaching the subject with

Heidi scares you a little, do some of the exercises we spoke about last year. Write it all down, everything you want to say, and see how it looks on paper.'

'I think I'll do that,' Nick said, and meant it. Though probably not the way Helen envisioned. 'I get the feeling there's something else?'

'There is. I've got the name here of someone you may want to meet when you get back. He's a post-doctoral at Harvard doing a series of lectures in Seattle. Nick, Mr. Denis has been studying sleep paralysis since 2015, and thinks science is finally catching up with the variables – the kind of things that can predict an episode. Would you be interested in having a discussion with him? Perhaps even volunteering for one of his studies before he goes home?'

Nick agreed. Though he suddenly felt deflated. While Helen's motive was understandable – this was an admittance on her part that she lacked the expertise to provide adequate help – it was still disappointing to know she was seeking a scientific rationalization. Yes, a post-doctorate would almost certainly believe his subjects were seeing apparitions. But his methodology for extracting any kind of diagnoses would be monitoring the amygdala portion of his brain. On the off-chance Nick brought his photographs (the ones he was beginning to think contained incontrovertible proof), there was a high degree of likelihood Mr. Denis would label him a clever hoaxer.

Manipulating illusions were (after all) Nick's stock in trade.

And what if I threw a wildcard like Saul Kidman into mix? Try to reason with a team of doctors that a person who didn't really exist tried to seduce me to the dark side?

When Nick returned, there would be no conference with any professional, post-doctorate or otherwise.

Unsurprisingly, Helen seemed to sense the dishonesty.

Before writing up his anti-depressant medication and saying her farewells, she favored Nick with a secretive look that spoke volumes: *If your only cure exists out there in Deception Pass ... then you go back and find it.*

***

The next morning, with his wife and daughter once again AWOL (this time on a shopping expedition that would take up most of the day), Nick sat down at his kitchen table to write a letter. For the task, he would be employing pen and paper. His laptop, already stowed away in its carry case, sat next to the front door with his other luggage.

After fifteen minutes of staring at nothing, he began to write.

Heidi,

Last night, I stayed up for hours thinking about what I would write – how to eloquently frame the proper words to explain this rash decision. But as I lay there, watching you sleep, I realized eloquence doesn't factor in concerning matters of the heart; it's all just purple prose attempting to articulate something primal. So, without further ado, let me come right out and say something I've been attempting to since that first night we shared a bed together (after the Soundgarden concert – remember?).

I've known for a long time that my condition will kill me. And I mean it, literally. There's no sugarcoating it or saying it any other way. Eventually, when all is said and done, you'll wake up beside me one morning to find me dead. This is not a supposition – or even superstition. It's a cold, hard fact ... one I have come to accept as rigidly as my own existence. This knowing came about a year after my brother died and hasn't abandoned me since. One day, very soon, the Shadows will find a means to stop my breathing. Strangely enough, I've gone on to learn this certainty is not uncommon among the tribe who experience sleep paralysis; they see the affliction no differently from a disease or an infection ... one whose fatality rate borders around one hundred percent.

Have I resigned myself to an early grave? Until recently, I will say yes. Despite putting on a brave face for my family, I have lived these many years of our marriage in a state of perpetual fear; so ingrained, it's become a species of tired acceptance. Slowly, this acquiescence to defeat became even more terrifying than the paralysis itself. So ... what has changed, if anything? Recent events, of course. While the accident didn't open a doorway into the afterlife, I was granted something equally mysterious: a retreading of the past, where I got to relive events and emotions most of us relegate to the amnesia of history. And the lesson of the experience was plain: there is a chance I don't have to die; I have a doorway of opportunity to let go of my resignation. For the first time in years, I feel a sliver of hope where there was none before; where I might have a future with you and Hayley and grow to be old.

Do you realize the miracle of this? There is HOPE. Though, it requires a confrontation of sorts. What kind, you ask? I'm not entirely sure of that myself. I only know where it will take place:

Deception Pass.

In those rugged blue waters hides a cove where the walls between worlds are thin.

You've probably decided by now this is something I must do alone. And you're right. But why?

Because anything of value worth saving has a price attached.

I know your first instinct will be to follow me. Please don't. Stay here with our daughter until I return.

I love you guys – more than anything.

Nick

***

To make sure his wife would be the one to read it, Nick decided to place the letter on top of their shared bureau. Before locking up the house, he made a final detour into his studio ... and collected the last photos taken from inside the Canlis building.

4

For the Wheeler clan, circa the 1980s, navigating to places afar was often a trying affair. With no GPS and only sun-parched maps, their drives to Whidbey Island invariably led to failed shortcuts and petty arguments. Father Chad, who on occasion exhibited a philosophical worldview, was of the opinion such fallouts were almost a rite of passage for the average American family.

Nick, armed with a glove-compartment of physical maps in addition to his Honda's GPS, encountered no such tribulations finding his way up the west coast. Upon arriving at the Mukilteo-Clinton Ferry under a burnished sky, Nick's car was promptly uploaded with a gaggle of other sightseers taking the scenic jaunt to Anacortes or Oak Harbor. Paying the toll with his credit card, Nick decided to forego any luxuries (including the ferry's onboard restaurant) lest this entire expedition eventually bankrupt him.

Though, that's not the real reason you won't get out. Admit it – you always sort of enjoyed this part of the journey.

While Louise and Sebastian couldn't wait to get above deck to spot wildlife, Nick was happiest remaining in the car, snug in one of two holding lots, staring out at white-capped waves and pondering another encounter with Saul Kidman. When they finally reached Island County, would Saul be in his usual spot, monitoring the same waves with his anti-reflective binoculars? Or would Nick be condemned to another solitary winter alone, his sole company thumbed copies of *Nexus* magazine?

Beside him, a voice said, 'You've been here before?'

Nick looked up ... and registered he'd neglected to shut the window. Beside it, gruff in the particulars, a bearded black man favored Nick with a toothless smile.

'I'm sorry?'

'I was asking if you've been this way before. You look like you have.'

A question, not a statement.

'I have,' Nick admitted. 'A long time ago.'

'You're coming during the off season; that usually gives it away.'

'Off season?'

The stranger regarded him through bloodshot eyes. 'No swimming or waterskiing this time of year. Not much of anything, really, except rain. So, why does anybody come unless they've been here before?'

'I suppose so. Do you live there?'

'Not anymore.'

Choosing not to clarify, the man fell silent ... though Nick could fill in the details. Permanent places in this part of the world were becoming rarer with every season, miles of real estate dotting the land regulated to the tourist trade.

Would Chad have pulled up stakes if his firstborn had lived? Nick wondered to himself. *I suppose not.*

'What was that?'

'Nothing,' Nick said. 'I was just speculating how much has changed.'

Revealing even more gums, the man brightened. 'I think you'll find things haven't changed at all. And that's the beauty of it, if you ask me. The nights are still long, and the days are always cloudy.'

More pleasantries ensued, and not long after, the man staggered back to his Chevy Impala. If the exchange was supposed to contain some kind of mystical import – the prodigal son's return christened with dire warnings – then Nick missed the subtext.

***

Two hours later, Nick was back on dry land. Before disembarking, he took a moment to study the wake of his passage, a reach of water spangled with so much orange it was almost umber. *I'm now on one of the longest islands in the continental United States,* he thought wryly. *No way off, except by boat.*

With this morose thought, Nick maneuvered his Honda past the straggling tourists.

Driving inland, he began to notice subtle signs of transformation almost everywhere. Roads – once narrow tracts of dirt – were now paved, asphalted, and (in some instances) widened. Gaudily arranged around new fences were even newer street signs and modern recreational areas. Only a half-mile from the cabin, fields of farmland were renovated to accommodate a local cemetery.

Cue the foreshadowing music ...

It was a small affair, and Nick may have

missed it entirely if not for having engaged the Honda's high beams. Written atop two overarching gates – gothic in design and decorated with padlocks – were the words *Deception Cemetery*. Rearing up in the charcoal dark were the ghostly suggestion of statues and gravestones.

Briefly, his recent dream resurfaced: skiing State Road 20 and passing the dead girl brandishing a sign.

'The Hat Man cometh,' Nick heard himself say aloud. Through the steering wheel, the Honda's dash was lit green with the onset of night. 'No, it's the Ferris Wheel who cometh, assholes. And guess what? He's all grown up.'

They were the kind of words that warranted some sort of ominous reply. Perhaps Nick would glimpse a Shadow specter in the Honda's headlights; perhaps he would hear the piggish bray of a cormorant ...

There was nothing.

A short time later, Nick pulled into the driveway of his childhood home, its renovated roof like a medieval church in the fading twilight.

***

The new owner, Greg Golden, was a local salmon fisherman who trusted a real estate office in

Seattle to handle check-ins for his Airbnb. Admittance inside (like everything else in the modern epoch) was entirely self-service. After unloading his one suitcase, all Nick had to do was type a provided security number into a keypad.

Nick stepped inside and (after a brief struggle) located light switches, thumbing one after the other. Abruptly, the cabin filled with enough light to throw everything – the lounge room, the hallway, even the edge of a kitchen island – into a stark and welcomed relief.

He thought: *How many people get to do this? Just how many humans in history have an opportunity to step into the same rooms they breathed in as a kid?*

Coupled with the sights were scents. Not the familiar scent of Wendy's perfume (Taboo) or little Bianca's kiddie bouquet – an intermingling of crayons and powder. No, this was the smell of holiday couples of a hundred different types: sipping wine and shagging; proposals, rejections, and tired arguments in front of a TV.

In short, a smell far removed from families.

Nick's phone, quiet for most of the trip, chose that moment to erupt. It would be Heidi, of course – wanting to know if he'd changed his mind. Wanting to know if he'd come home ...

'Hello, Nick,' came Greg Golden's voice

through the speaker. The owner of *Deception Tree House* sounded tipsy. 'Have you arrived? Did you manage to get in okay?'

'No problem,' Nick replied, depositing his meager luggage on the floor. He wondered why Greg would be calling when all heretofore exchanges, for the most part, had consisted of emails.

'Electricity working? Everything okay there?'

Surveying the main living area, Nick also took in the well-lit hallway with exposed ceiling beams. In addition to a central chandelier dominating the foyer, he spied two lamps placed around an assortment of furniture.

'It's all good. Why do you ask?'

A brief pause. Greg taking a sip of his chosen poison. 'A strong windstorm pushed through western Washington last week. A quarter of a million homes lost power, including mine. Can you believe a flying trampoline caught between power lines caused the damage? A friend of mine owns an eight-foot sailboat. When he woke up, it was on somebody's lawn.'

Picturing the trampoline, Nick held back laughter.

'And that's not half of it. In Coupeville, a black bear was spotted rearranging someone's birdfeeders.'

'Did you say *bear*?'

'I did. It's unique here ... but not unheard of. Bears are excellent swimmers.'

'He *swam* to the island?'

'He must have. And ate three pounds of bird food before moseying away.'

'Jeez.'

'Anyway, you shouldn't be worried. Any bears are long gone. Although, you might see some work crews still around, tidying up the area. I hope this doesn't impact your stay.'

'I couldn't see how it would.'

Greg coughed. Sounding embarrassed, he asked, 'Will anybody be joining you there?'

In earlier interactions, Nick failed to divulge living in the cabin once upon a time. And why should he? This return, pilgrimage, whatever you wanted to call it – was a personal endeavor.

Anybody else knowing his reasons for being here served no salient purpose.

'It's none of my business, of course,' the owner was saying. 'But you mentioned your stay might be a month ... even longer. And Deception Pass during the winter is probably not the best time to be isolated. Roads will close. Stores, too. Another storm like the one we just had might return for an encore performance.'

'I'm familiar with the area,' Nick said, hoping

a sliver of truth might placate the man.

Greg sounded more than relieved. 'You are? That's good. That's *very* good. Then you might know many of the houses close by have recently been sold off or demolished. Right now, Deception Tree House is *especially* remote. Do you happen to carry a firearm?'

Nick couldn't quite believe what he was hearing. 'Are you asking me to rethink my stay? Because if you are, you're doing a *really* good job.'

The owner sounded resentful at the idea.

'Of course not. As a Superhost, I just wanted to make sure everything will be okay. Enjoy your stay, Mr. Wheeler. Don't hesitate to call in the event you require help.'

***

Having unpacked his clothes, Nick set to the task of exploring. While the undertaking should have been a pleasant one, the owner's words left a portentous mark.

Many of the houses close by have been demolished.

Did this mean Nick was entirely free of neighbors?

Don't hesitate to call in the event you require help.

'Why not just come right out and tell me the

cabin is haunted, Greg?' Nick asked aloud. 'That's probably something a Superhost should mention.'

Until now, the cabin, a repository for lost souls, was something Nick had scarcely contemplated.

For his stay, Greg loaded the main fridge with various wines, both red and white. Pouring himself a generous helping of Sauvignon Blanc, Nick stopped motionless when something (a loud something) thumped in the attic space above.

Just wind coming down through the chimney. Don't jive to the haunted-house dance, Nick. Your ghosts have always been internal.

His glass filled, Nick wandered over to the chimney. Patterned with twisted filigrees of vine, the iron surround somehow managed to escape any modernization. And, aside from the addition of a Hudson sofa, almost nothing else was changed in this portion of the cabin, either. While no doubt going through many steam cleanings, the carpet below was the same versatile beige, unchanged with a changing of the guard.

But alternations reigned elsewhere.

Including a newly installed stairway leading to a second floor.

Walking them, Nick could see a balcony before reaching the summit: a thin terrace accessed by glass doors, the roof itself in the shape of a pyramidal tree.

The second floor contained one giant room lined with built-in bookcases. A covered billiard table served as its centerpiece.

To think, every drama of the Wheeler family happened right under my feet.

Nick's nose, attuned to the smells of fresh carpet and paint, suddenly caught a whiff of something unmistakable: Old Spice cologne.

Old Spice was Chad Wheeler's chosen aftershave.

Added to this was a yeasty odor – one evocative of corn chips.

Nick recognized it as the smell of Sebastian's feet, an ever-present aroma in and around their shared bedroom.

Impossible, of course.

Nick's olfactory senses, assaulted by this homecoming, conjured Old Spice and Sebastian's feet from memory.

Outside the triangular doors, night leaned in as a black and physical barrier. Like something glimpsed through smoke, Nick's Honda stood as a jagged slash of white against the dark.

Those doors have an Amityville vibe, he thought. *I'll be damned if they don't.*

Despite the holiday surrounds, Nick felt himself shiver.

***

Next, Nick investigated the laundry and bathroom (nothing untoward and everything in its place), then peeked into Chad and Wendy's old room, befitted with a four-poster bed and antique furniture. For better or worse, it was just a room, and as Nick returned to the hallway, no familiar scents followed him.

Endeavoring to open the room he used to call his own, Nick discovered it locked.

Turning the knob did not provide access. Nor did leaning his weight against the panels and pushing. Somebody – either Greg or a professional cleaner – locked this door with a key.

Nothing online suggested any rooms would be sealed off.

Nick had driven eighty miles to stay in his old bedroom ... and the way was barred.

Whatever's in there will still be waiting for you tomorrow. Drink your wine and get some shuteye.

Sage advice – because tomorrow entailed exploring outside.

While the main bedroom seemed a logical choice to sleep, Nick settled instead for the Hudson sofa. Fortified with Sauvignon Blanc – and central heating – his first night in Deception Pass would hopefully prove to be an uneventful one.

***

Awoken by something, Nick flailed in the darkness. A moment of panic ensued after discovering no Heidi slumbering by his side.

Recalling everything, Nick felt a knife-thrust of fear. The proverbial scared-of-the-dark kind.

What the hell was I thinking, coming back here alone?

From the window, the sound came again: tapping.

It demanded Nick look. And so, he did.

Deceased for thirty years, Sebastian Wheeler stared into the living room.

In death, Sebastian retained his youthful appearance: a freckled nose set under a mop of brown hair. Also visible through the glass was the collar of Sebastian's blue pajamas; the same ones he purchased with birthday money the year before.

The year before I killed him.

Returning Sebastian's stare, Nick comprehended a fundamental role-reversal at play. An age ago, *Nick* had been the one standing outside and looking in.

Holding up a finger, Sebastian tapped the glass again.

Then it came to Nick. Right this second, he was *inside* an episode. Not quite asleep ... yet not fully awake, either. Instead of staving off the inevitable with wine, this was something he should have prepared for.

In lieu of Shadows, Sebastian had come knocking.

Can I move, though?

Looking down, Nick watched his fingers play nothing but air.

His neck was also up to task.

Not an episode.

Sebastian's eyes glittered in the night, imploring.

Nick closed his eyes again ... and kept them shut. As he often did during bad episodes, praying came naturally.

After a full minute, he opened them again.

No one stood outside the window.

Palpable relief, a weight lifted. Pulling himself upright, he managed to stand. Slowly, he took a step forward.

And collided with last night's wine, tipping the bottle over.

Halfway to the window, Nick froze again.

Dark figures stood in the driveway.

Silhouettes in the shape of men.

Poised, Nick waited for the delayed reaction of paralysis to catch up with his conscious self.

You can still move.

So, whatever's out there must be real.

Only a thin gauze of white material, the window's curtains did not obstruct anything that might otherwise be visible with the naked eye.

The Honda, parked at an angle, lay enveloped in a skein of fog.

Wrapped in a kind of militaristic garb, two men faced the cabin. Their faces, unseen and unreadable, took on transparency as Nick inched closer.

Almond eyes with no mouths.

For the first time ever, he felt a different kind of paralysis: fear providing the impetus to be still. If he decided to move now, the shapes outside would use the seconds to cover the distance to the cabin.

This time, Nick, concentrating on his heartbeat, employed a counting measure Heidi had shown him in the early days. These apparitions, while viewed in a waking state, were surely no different from the countless others he glimpsed in this cabin as a child.

Wait them out, and they'll disappear.

After a while, he *did* begin to relax. Though anticipating commotion outside, there was nothing to hear but a stagnant wind blowing against the eaves.

Nick reached fifty. Then seventy. With three digits approaching, he opened his eyes and stared out the window.

To be greeted by the same almond-eyed

apparitions, their bodies now pressed firmly up against the window; those implacable eyes reserved solely for the man cowering inside.

5

Nick awoke, his mouth tasting like a latrine. Through the curtains, a gray dawn heralded the first spatters of wind-driven snow.

A mouth tasting like a latrine – one of Wendy's euphemisms for a hangover. How'd I ever forget that one?

It was the cabin, of course, working its subtle magic. Opening a repository of memories that were (up until now) buried within his subconscious mind like a vault of photographs. First, the scent of Old Spice. Then, Sebastian's feet. And during the night ...

Memories flooded back: Sebastian at the window, his dark eyes demanding. And soon after, figures standing nonchalantly in the driveway. Though humanoid in shape, their eyes told an altogether different story.

Like aliens ...

During his adolescence, there was a time when Nick had taken an almost scholastic approach to his sleep paralysis, studying everything he could about a poorly understood subject that was seemingly as old as the species itself. In dozens of cultures – if not hundreds – men and women described falling asleep, waking up, and thereafter being unable to move their bodies. They illustrated Shadow beings using a person's helplessness to instill some kind of fundamental terror in which to feed. Oftentimes, these creatures bore more than a passing resemblance to the almond-eyed aliens so prolific in western culture; the androgynous beings who world-hopped on UFOs and probed the unwary human body, physically and spiritually. While their emergence into the modern zeitgeist morphed into a running punchline, Nick was completely captivated by those ominous eyes. So enthralled, in fact, that he would later convince himself his episodes were at the behest of alien beings. Saul Kidman, the strange enigma who prowled these environs, had planted this seed early on, insisting their sightings together on the slope were craft from other dimensions or planets. Finally solved, the enigma of sleep paralysis was nothing more than a colossal smokescreen for another species to assault the human race under the curtain of night.

While the abduction phenomenon was an attractive explanation for a time, he eventually put the notion away. Yes, many Shadow creatures *did* resemble aliens, but this in no way proved they were.

Then what did I see at the curtain last night?

Dissimilar from the usual suspects, Nick's newest visitors had indeed been in keeping with the Gray alien: dark eyes devoid of pupils, the skin like leather or hide. Seeing them up close – outside the realm of sleep – must have been cause enough for Nick to lose consciousness.

Or perhaps something altogether different was at work.

Perhaps 'missing time' could now be added to Nick's catalogue of terrors.

***

Despite the ominous nature of the night (in addition to a mild hangover), Nick was in good spirits as daybreak gave way to midmorning. Away from the raucous din of a teenager getting ready – and Heidi's predilection to play Taylor Swift – the interior silence of the cabin was a godsend. Wind was prevalent, of course, moaning through layers of insulation like a mournful psalm. But this elegy, both somber and poignant, only served to make Nick feel more at ease.

By 10:30am, thoughts of specters had vanished.

Long and languid, his shower was augmented with a giant breakfast consisting of hash browns and diced gourmet sausages on a three-tiered English muffin. Over the course of their marriage, his wife gravitated toward a subtle form of veganism, often substituting plant-based alternatives in lieu of livestock. And, while those surrogates were often on par with their real cousins, Greg Golden's gourmet brand illustrated an acute disparity.

'Like the difference between matter and antimatter,' Nick said around a mouthful of muffin. 'Matter in this instance being the pig.'

After breakfast, Nick played himself in a game of pool. With no one around to critique his style, he pocketed balls with the confidence of a pro. Then it was onto the balcony, which provided an invigorating view of the neighboring hinterland obscured the previous night. Mount Rainier, barely perceptible even on clear days, brooded above a halo of gray cloud. Once planted and arrayed as fencing, the yellow larch trees had been stripped back to accommodate only meagre saplings.

Perhaps if I squint hard enough, I'll be able to

see my path ...

Wishful thinking.

If he wanted evidence the path was still around, he would have to go down there and find it.

***

Before leaving, Nick filled a backpack with sandwiches and a thermos of coffee. Though determined to abstain from taking pictures during his stay – the sight of his camera arsenal felt too much like work – he pocketed a Canon PowerShot at the last minute.

His first pitstop: the end of the driveway where apparitions had stood.

Nick navigated the earth as though the land were littered with grenades.

Nothing. Not so much as a footprint.

The morning's snowstorm, though brief, covered evidence of any phantoms.

He took pictures, anyway, hoping to uncover something later when uploading them.

Maybe they were human?

Nick briefly considered that possibility: the chance that someone, tipped off regarding his stay, decided to don a trench coat and scare him witless.

Someone aware of his identity.

Minor curiosities in the '80s, his family became

more notorious after Sebastian's fall. Even Saul's slope, a previously unremarkable hillock, was christened a pilgrimage sight for the morbidly curious.

So, is it outside the realm of possibility that some individual, knowing you've come home to roost, has taken it upon themselves to wreak havoc on your personal life and safety?

Feeling suddenly vulnerable outside in the open, Nick meditated on returning to the slope. If somebody *was* observing his movements, perhaps throwing them a curveball would make things more interesting.

That narrow portion of land, scoured and weathered by time, would still be waiting for him tomorrow.

Today, another part of the island called.

***

Among the gravestones, a solitary figure wandered.

Having approached the cemetery from the rear, Nick expected it to be as devoid of people as the previous night. Not wanting to engage the mourner, he briefly considered fleeing back to the cabin.

Too late, she already looked in his direction.

It's a she alright. Someone around my age.

The cemetery, flanked by a descending pathway, was maintained with an extraordinary level of upkeep – lavender and vegetation provided the illusion of a small valley. Built on an elevated prairie, Nick could easily imagine Hobbit holes dotting the landscape.

It sprung up just as we left. Good thing, too. Wendy might have insisted Sebastian be interred here.

An unbidden image of his brother rose up: Sebastian tapping casually at the window ...

The sound of the mourner's voice drifted over.

Nick registered it wasn't aimed in his direction. Wandering only three rows away, she was speaking into a cell phone.

He was looking at a ginger-haired woman in her mid-forties. Dourly dressed, her eyes were hidden by sunglasses.

When the call ended, she pocketed her phone and glanced in his direction.

'It's you, isn't it, Nick?' she asked. 'Oh Lord, I *thought* it might be.'

He stood slack jawed.

'It was your gait,' the woman went on. 'I recognized that slouch from a mile away. Nicholas. It *really* is you.'

Then it was upon him ... even before her sunglasses were removed, revealing shamrock eyes.

'Rosa?' he blurted; his shock absolute. '*Rosa* Collins?'

'It's me, Nick.'

***

Their embrace, awkward at first, quickly became something more intimate.

'Look at you,' he said when they finally untangled. 'All grown up.'

'Look at *you*,' Rosa replied, the suggestion of tears in her green eyes. 'The last time I saw you, you had one of those bad teenage moustaches.'

'I did?'

A hand reached up and delicately stroked his left cheek. 'I can't believe you're standing in front of me. What are you doing here? I thought you and your family lived in the city?' Seeing the confusion on his face, Rosa added, 'The Internet can be your friend if you want to stalk someone.'

'So, you must have seen –'

'What you do for a living? I glanced at it.' Rosa smiled. 'Relax. It's no big deal. I got the impression you're someone who wanted to make B-grade horror but settled for photography instead.'

And just like that, Rosa had (for the most part) unpacked the truth. More often than not, those new to his work regarded the subject matter of his pictures to be the art of an unbalanced mind.

'You're never going to believe this,' he said. 'But I'm staying in the old place.'

Nick elucidated: after sustaining minor injuries in a work-related accident, he sought a chance to heal away from home. And, purely by accident, stumbled upon the cabin's present incarnation as a holiday locale.

'It's half as cheap during the winter,' he said, hoping to downplay any paranormal inference by dismantling the mundane aspects. 'Of course, it's geared toward couples now. There's a second floor and even a chandelier. Still, if I'm going to recuperate anywhere, why not do it in a place that holds significant memories?'

Rosa's smile wavered. Nick could sense her wrestling the import of his decision. Significant memories? No doubt, she was wondering how much he remembered. Which beggared the question: How much did *she*?

And how much had she chosen to forget?

Rosa said, 'I read about your accident. It made the *Seattle Times*. Are you still in any pain? You seem fine.'

'I am. Miraculously so. But what about you? Are *you* still living in the same place? My host said something about some of the houses being demolished.'

'Our place is still there. Mine and Mitchell's.

We inherited it when Mom passed away.'

Vague snatches of Chrissie Collins filtered through. 'I'm sorry to hear that. You live with your brother?'

'We did. For many years, but not anymore.'

'Where is Mitchell now?'

'Here. Three rows over, to be precise. Being so close, I can visit him at least once a week.'

Fifteen seconds went by before Nick grasped the implication. Mitchell Collins, the bigger boy Nick once decreed a bully, now had a permanent home here in the cemetery.

'How did –'

'Mitchell was a troubled man, Nick. He was partially the reason I stayed on the island. He needed care. Mitchell ... developed problems not long after your family left. Sleeping problems and mental health issues. I guess in my own way, I developed them, too. But I learned how to cope far better than Mitchell.'

These revelations raised a whole gamut of questions, none of which Nick was prepared to ask.

Maybe, it's just as you feared. Maybe Rosa developed her own form of sleep paralysis after your time together in the caves ... Maybe, they both did.

The alternative – Mitchell Collins had taken his own life due to mental illness – was somehow even more depressing.

'Rosa ...' he began and didn't know how to proceed. Mitchell's final resting place, a small wonderland upon entrance, suddenly felt oppressive.

Sensing his struggle, Rosa said, 'Not now, Nick. How long are you going to be staying on the island?'

Having little idea what his response would be, Nick heard himself saying, 'Sebastian's anniversary is approaching. Probably until Christmas.'

As if she anticipated his response, Rosa simply nodded.

'Why don't I come over soon? Say tomorrow? I'll bring wine and ... there's just so much we need to discuss.'

***

It was cold when Nick awoke.

Dark and insufferably cold.

No comforter covered his midsection; no cushions plied his back.

He lay on a hard surface.

Wind stung his nostrils and hair.

I'm not on the couch. I'm not even inside.

The realization caused him to jerk upright, hard pebbles biting into the surface of his palms. Riding coattails with the cold was a sharp scent, alkaline and unmistakable.

Seawater.

Close by came a rhythmical susurration: the sound of waves.

To stave off panic, Nick tried to piece together his last movements. Earlier, there was his chance encounter with Rosa. After making plans to see her again, he returned to the cabin, his sole ambition to imbibe more wine and read his Kindle. As darkness settled, Nick retired to the Hudson sofa early, confident enough booze coursed through his system to put him out of commission until morning.

Not so. You've managed to sleepwalk to the edge of a fucking cliff.

Not just any cliff, either... *the* cliff. The one where Sebastian met his fate.

Enough moonlight was visible to illuminate familiar bulges of land. Only ten feet away lay the incline, blades of grass tipped with ice. On Nick's right, their branches thrashing like kelp in a tide, were the Douglas fir trees so pertinent to this strange slope of land.

Everything is here and accounted for ...

Except for Saul Kidman, of course.

Surveying the dark, Nick fully expected the man to emerge at any moment. Surely, Saul performed this summons, ushering Nick away from the comfort of his couch like a munificent pied piper.

The wind howled.

The trees sang.

But Saul did not appear.

If you don't get off this slope, you'll freeze.

A minute passed ... and Nick, at last, stood upright. Drunkenly, he staggered forward, intent on finding his path. By the time it came into being, a twisting thoroughfare of black and gray, new snow had begun to fall.

***

When the cabin appeared, Nick had been walking for perhaps thirty minutes. His relief (knowing he would soon be warm again) was augmented by lights burning on the upper floor.

Did I leave them on?

It was feasible.

But highly improbable.

Through the windows, humanoid shapes moved.

This far away, through a gauze of sleet, there was no way to determine their origin. Had the trench-coat mafia returned for a second successive night? Had they decided on a game of pool while the owner was out sleepwalking?

Perhaps, it's Sebastian who's returned?

Eyes fixed on the windows; Nick crossed the lawn. If sleepwalking was indeed the villain here, then Nick in all probability left the front door wide open, an invitation to anything or anyone to step through.

With a hunched, drooping posture that was unambiguously human, a dark silhouette pressed itself against the balcony doors. On its left, a smaller version joined it. Then another on the right.

Linking arms, they stared out at the night, seemingly as aware of the man on the lawn as he of them.

Get out. Go back to the main road if you have to. You're not equipped to deal with this.

But was this altogether true? Nick's decision to return to Deception Pass had been entirely premeditated, without proviso. Reserving the cabin, he'd known full well that ghosts, in all likelihood, had a permanent home here. And never mind his condition, either – because whether he liked to admit it or not, his memories of the Shadows were firmly entrenched in the real world.

You not only signed on the dotted line – you laid out the fucking welcome mat.

Purposefully, Nick strode across the remaining grass, taking the steps carefully. They, like Greg Golden's generic doormat, were covered in a fine dusting of snow.

The front door was open.

Missing time and now sleepwalking, he thought, sidestepping the mat and closing the door. *Pretty soon, Shadow Men will be the least of your –*

Parallel with the kitchen island, Nick froze. Once more, he smelled aftershave: Old Spice, to be precise.

As if the scent were a harbinger, Nick heard a voice emanating from the end of the hallway.

A human voice.

A perpetual constant in the cabin, the wind had the propensity to mimic the baritone command of a human voice box. More than once, Nick remembered his father pointing this out. However, what carried to his ears now was no more the wind than the sound of his bare feet slapping the floorboards.

A woman's cadence floated on the air, rising with the inflection of someone in debate.

'*I felt scared. I've never been scared like that before. Chad ... he ...*'

Closing his eyes, Nick willed the auditory delusion away.

'*... almost like he's passed it on. How else to explain what I've been seeing?*'

Stairs to the second floor shimmered in Nick's field of sight, a distorted mirage. Going up them wasn't an option, of course ... because Nick had to investigate the origin of the voice.

A voice that was undeniably … Wendy Fuller's.

'Imagination, Wendy. You know how dark it gets here. How easy it is to see things that aren't there.'

Sounding youthful and somber, Chad Wheeler.

Nick's feet carried him forward, toward the bedrooms. With every step, he expected the voices to vanish, but their pitch only increased.

'... maybe I'm the one who should be seeing a doctor. Chad, some nights I wake up terrified.'

Only the kitchen light penetrated this portion of hallway, enough so that Nick's shadow crossed the threshold of Chad and Wendy's old room before Nick did.

Were you expecting some kind of reaction?

Nick realized he had been. Sensing, then seeing his shadow, his patriarchal stepmother would demand Nick step into the room and reveal himself.

Wendy Fuller, despite the notable handicap of being confined to a retirement village, still wielded her villainous influence.

Nick stepped into the bedroom, flicked on the light.

Empty.

A goose-down quilt, untouched since his arrival

and pulled taut at the corners of the room's four-poster bed, contained the distinctive impression of a person.

'I did that,' Nick whispered. 'When I peeked into the room last night.'

But he hadn't.

Seeing the room so clean, so pristine, Nick backed away without so much as a glance at the furniture.

His overriding thought (that this was still his father's bedroom and therefore off-limits) had been as pervasive as the lingering, physical smell of his aftershave.

Suddenly, another smell filled Nick's nose; one that was like a cousin to an old man's cologne: Taboo perfume, the staple brand of stepmothers everywhere.

Feeling as if he *would* faint, Nick stepped back into the hallway.

Then heard footsteps bounding across the ceiling, a hurried scampering from the second floor.

***

Before going upstairs, Nick mentally replayed the sound. Like a child skipping, the dirge caused windows to shake. Surely, whatever he'd glimpsed through the second-floor windows outside –

paralysis shadows or the new threat from last night – were not the architects of such simple mischief.

This is ridiculous. I've become the heroine of a fucking Susan Hill novel. How long before the Angel of Death makes an appearance?

His fears allayed, seeing the second floor in darkness, Nick proceeded to inspect every corner; hoping to uncover any evidence this delirium wasn't the result of a fragmented mind. And just like the driveway outside, he found nothing.

Covered in tarp after his morning's exertions, the pool table was a black bulk in the shape of a coffin.

'I might be losing my mind,' he said, and – though his words were met with silence, Nick got the impression the cabin was agreeing with him.

I'm hearing the voices of people still alive.

Which meant … what, exactly? If the cabin wasn't haunted in any traditional sense, what the hell was going on?

Then something dawned on him: a hollow theory smacking of undeniable truth.

You heard a conversation between Wendy and Chad you were never supposed to hear. Just call it what it was: the past. Your stepmother was talking about seeing things ... the same things she said were all in your head.

Once downstairs again, Nick felt a powerful

headache settling in.

This was too much to think about, too much to absorb.

His phone, untouched since earlier in the evening, revealed dawn was near. If Nick wanted a clear head when Rosa arrived, a few more hours of uninterrupted sleep would be necessary.

She's someone who's been touched by the mystery. Tell her the truth about everything. There's a possibility she'll believe you.

It was a comforting thought. And it somehow made perfect sense. Once upon a time, Rosa had briefly been his ally in this madness. Maybe, she could be again.

Returning to the living room, Nick discovered his laptop on a side table, powered up and humming away. Before turning in, he'd placed the computer in hibernation mode.

This development, in a night that included sleepwalking to Saul's slope, hardly seemed surprising.

Bending down, Nick observed a flashing cursor in the top corner of an opened document.

Five separate words had been typed in italicized caps.

Five words meant as four.

WEL COME HOME, FERRIS WHEEL.

6

Having spied Rosa's journey across the driveway, Nick had the door wide open as she mounted the steps. For the occasion, he'd dressed in a long-sleeved chambray shirt over a striped tee.

'I should have passed on my cell number yesterday,' he said, ushering her inside with a polite wave.

'So you could have texted me and cancelled?'

Nick laughed. 'So you could have texted *me* and cancelled. Or for anything else. For instance, I could have saved you the trouble of bringing any wine. We're completely covered in that area.'

Rosa brandished her bottle. 'This? It's a 2015 Californian vintage for the purpose of being polite.

Never arrive anywhere emptyhanded was drilled into me from a young age.'

Taking the proffered bottle, Nick led them through the foyer and into the kitchen. Arranged on its island were a startling array of canapés brimming with foodstuffs.

'You've been busy,' Rosa said, clearly impressed.

'I hardly lifted a finger, believe it or not. My Superhost Greg – that's what he calls himself, a Superhost – made sure I'd want for nothing. Help yourself. Some of this stuff ... see that salmon there? Some of it I'll end up throwing out if you don't partake. Red or white?'

'Red, please. You're not a fan of fish, I take it?'

Pouring, Nick said, 'No. And I think I know the reason why. It was growing up here, being so close to all the fishing boats. My brother used to tease me about fish being full of mercury – and stuff we haven't even discovered yet. Looking back, I think he was just trying to freak me out, the way kids do. And I guess it worked.'

Smiling, Rosa accepted her glass ... and Nick took a brief second to appreciate the moment. Also dressed somewhat formally (cropped trousers, a black blouse, and light jewelry), the girl of his childhood had grown into a beautiful, full-bodied woman. Nick's prologue dream of coming here – a

nightmare featuring Rosa as a sign-carrying corpse
– proved to be no more portentous than the old man
on the ferry.

*Deception Pass, for all its strange ambiguity, is
really just full of deception ...*

'What is it?' Rosa asked.

'It's like you said yesterday ... I just can't
believe you're standing here in front of me.'

'We're lucky in that regard, don't you think? I
mean, what were the chances your cabin would be
available to rent? Your wife and daughter ... will
they be joining you here?'

Nick felt himself flinch, and Rosa held up a
hand. 'It's none of my business. Only that you're
alone and –'

'No, you're right to ask. Yesterday, you *also*
mentioned there was a lot we needed to talk about.
So ... let's go up to the balcony and talk.'

***

Before traversing the stairs, Nick made sure
their glasses were full and a bottle was in hand.

'It's strange to think,' Nick said. 'But I never
invited you over here when we were kids, did I?'

'We weren't friends for long, Nick. Oh ... look
at this!'

In preparation for Rosa's arrival, Nick opened

the balcony doors. Afternoon sunlight – Whidbey Island's strange version of it – flooded every corner of the second floor in dust-laden shafts of yellow and gold.

'They've given the house a name,' Nick said. 'Deception Tree House.'

'I can see why,' said Rosa, stepping onto the balcony and inhaling the day. 'It's shaped like a Christmas tree. And those windows –'

'Feel like eyes?'

'And ... I can almost see Mount Rainier! It's remote, but there. Nick, you're very lucky. This is beautiful.'

Thinking of the humanoid apparitions from last night, Nick thought: *Come dark, you may not think so, my dear.*

'Shall we sit?'

Rosa cast a glance at Greg Golden's sparse outdoor furniture, which consisted of two polymer chairs. 'Let's stand. This is the part where we exchange pleasantries.'

Placing his elbows on the balcony railing, Nick said, 'You've seen what I do for a living, but what about you? Do you still hate Saturdays here as much as I remember?'

Rosa grinned. 'I *love* Saturdays. The mornings, anyway. Mornings are devoted to my students.'

'You teach?'

'Of a type.'

Rosa held out her left hand for him to peruse. 'See those calluses? That's twenty years of strumming an acoustic. I advertise locally, and people from all over the island come to my place to be taught the basics. Weekdays are devoted to my own compositions.'

'You're a tutor and a songwriter?'

Nodding coyly, Rosa said, 'Being a musician, forging an atypical music career, wasn't something I gave serious thought to until my early thirties. But now, everything's changed. These days, if you have a decent YouTube channel and a Patreon page, people will pay you money.'

'Country?'

Rosa nudged his arm. 'Nothing so passé. If I could compare my songs to any artist alive today, it would probably be Alanis Morissette. My best tunes go up on Soundcloud. Anything midrange, I'll put up for free. While it's a shifting era for musicians, I embrace the freedom it offers. No touring; no shady managers, either. Best of all, I can stay right here on the island.'

Standing and talking, Nick's sudden urge for a cigarette was overpowering. Though he seldom smoked outside of parties, the twin accelerants of wine and conversation were always triggers.

He said, 'I guess I was always curious about

that part. When did you move here permanently?'

'It would have been ... let's see. Early '98.'
Rosa's smile broadened. 'When Alanis Morissette
was *all* the rage. By then, Mom owned the place
freehold. And after she passed, I thought, why not?
Coming back, it's like your memory of everything
reasserts itself. I can recall *everything* like it was
yesterday.'

Now, we're getting somewhere.

'And your memories of us?' Nick asked.

'A girl doesn't forget her first crush, Nick. So
... I think this concludes the pleasantries part; don't
you think? Should we move onto more serious
subjects?'

Nick studied his guest. Though Rosa's smile
still held firm, it was now lent a serious bent.

'Last night,' he said. 'I couldn't sleep. No
surprises there. And I remember thinking that I
wanted to share everything with you today – that
talking it through would help. The moment's
arrived and ...'

'You could listen to me talk about Alanis
Morissette all day?'

'Yes.'

Pointedly, Rosa finished off what remained in
her glass. After a moment studying the horizon, she
said, 'Another one, please. And one for you, too.
We're going to need it.'

***

'You introduced me to a world of monsters,' Rosa said. 'And I don't begrudge you for it.'

Nick had no immediate retort. He expected a revelation, yes – but didn't quite anticipate Rosa's candid tact. Though the statement introduced a whole slew of questions, Nick simply waited for what came next.

'That's something I've been wanting to get off my chest since yesterday. It was right after we hugged ... I could sense, *feel*, that you carry a lot of guilt inside you.'

'I do,' Nick admitted. 'If I hadn't –'

'It was *my* idea to explore the cave, remember? In fact, I practically dragged you along for the ride. You were on your way to see your friend, and I intercepted.'

'Saul ...' Nick said and let the word hang.

'Yes, *him*.'

'It's not what happened that day that really concerns me,' Nick said. 'When you said a world of *monsters*. Did you mean –'

'That you somehow passed on your affliction?' Rosa barked out surprised laughter. 'Nothing as dramatic as that, Nick. Let me put your mind to rest in that regard. Do I sometimes *dream* about what happened to us in the cave? Occasionally, I do. And some nights I wake dripping sweat, an afterimage of orange clouds and black glass burning behind my eyelids.'

'What about paralysis? Not being able to move your body? Do you ever ...' Nick swallowed. 'Do you ever see Shadows?'

Rosa shook her head, and Nick could see the patient guitar teacher in her expression. 'I never did. You could say I escaped them ... by learning how.'

While Nick felt unadorned relief knowing Rosa had been spared, his overall guilt was far from assuaged.

He said, 'I'm scared to know what that means.'

'My mom had a saying,' Rosa continued. 'Playing possum. You've heard of it? It basically means playing dead. And that's what I did in the weeks following what happened. I remembered how mad you were with me for letting it slip we went down there, so part of it was for you. Another part was to stop my mother and Mitchell's interrogating questions. After a few months went by, they *did* stop. And that's when I began to search for answers of my own.'

Knowing where this might be heading, Nick asked, 'Sort of like a personal mission?'

'You remember how I hated Saturdays? Well, I began to use them. Not to return to the tunnel, though. I never found the courage to go back there again. No, I began walking to the Oak Harbor Library. To rifle through their collection of encyclopedias dealing with the supernatural.'

Nick, who had devoted a lifetime to novice research, nodded his understanding.

'There were the usual suspects to look at,' Rosa said. 'Things like telepathy and telekinesis – which I already knew from TV shows. The topic of Shadow people, though? That was a lot harder to find.'

Especially back then, Nick thought. *If it weren't for Saul and his magazines, I would have been completely lost.*

'There were sketches by Native Americans that reflected some of what we saw,' Rosa said. 'Religious folklore offered up their jinns and shades of the underworld. I saw drawings of them, too. Apparitions with little structure. The more I looked, the more I began to see patterns across every culture. Tales going back to early Islam told of demons capable of possessing people who slept alone. One Anglo-Swiss artist, Henry Fuseli, produced an oil painting –'

'*The Nightmare*?'

Rosa shook her head vigorously. 'Yes! *The Nightmare*. The one depicting an apelike Incubus crouching on the chest of a hapless female. When I first saw it, I felt like all the pieces of a jigsaw were finally coming together.'

Nick said, 'It's thought to be one of the first physical representations of the Night Hag, or a Shadow Demon. Described by early sufferers of sleep paralysis.'

'God, those two words together ... sleep *and* paralysis. I brooded on them nightly. Scared that my sleuthing would somehow bring attention to me.'

'From whom?'

'From your friend, Saul, for one. Though, I never spotted him again after you left. And from ... other things. The ones I was reading about. Nick, you were brave that day in the cave. Telling me what it was like for you. How you suffered.'

Vague snatches of the past filtered through: Rosa ahead in the dark and barely discernible; Nick unburdening himself of secrets, wanting Rosa prepared for the literal and figurative darkness ahead.

Nick said, 'I'm sorry.'

'Whatever for?'

'For what happened ... afterward. For the way I treated you.'

You gave her the cold shoulder. And not only on that day. You brushed her aside when she was trying to help you. To warn you about Saul.

'We were scared kids, Nick.'

'What about your mom ... did she let things

go?'

'Chrissie Collins was too booze-addled to care much. Mitchell, though. He was a different story. You see, he blamed you. He was, I don't know, seeking a scapegoat for the island's ills. What happened to your brother, he assumed you were somehow responsible. After your family left Whidbey, he would occasionally corner me, demanding to know the precise details of our time together.'

'And?'

'And I never told him anything.'

'Never?'

'Not even toward the end of his life.'

'And how did he ...'

'A kind of bloodstream infection,' Rosa replied, her tone almost bland. 'Septicemia. He had a mild addiction to opiates that increased the risk and brought it on. Initially, we thought it was just the flu. Mitchell ... he was never one for hospitals. That was two years ago.'

'Jesus,' Nick said, and couldn't offer up anything else. In the cemetery, Rosa hinted Mitchell's mental health may also have had some role to play, but Nick wasn't ready to go there yet.

'I didn't want to believe the specifics about sleep paralysis at first,' Rosa was saying, as if the subject of her brother was just as taboo as Nick's own. 'That it could induce such terrors. And if *you* were the focal point, why did *I* see those terrors, too? This led me to seeking another explanation, fringe stuff a younger me would never have considered.'

Nick hazarded a guess. 'You wanted to know if delusions could be shared?'

'Precisely! Of course, I would go on to learn they *could* be. And the French, they even have a name for –'

'Folie à deux,' Nick said. 'The Madness of Two.'

'Yes! Delusions transmitted from one person to another, like a virus. The phenomenon is rare, yet completely real. Anyway, the syndrome is usually shared between two people with a special bond, like siblings.'

'You were a friend to me during a time when I had none, except for Saul. But it's like you said, we weren't exactly buddies for long.'

'Which threw the whole *special bond* thing for me out the window. And left only one real possibility. I decided that your Shadow creatures were real. Real monsters with real intent. And the place we saw underground ... their *metropolis*. I decided that was *also* real. As real and tangible as *this* world.'

Nick felt speechless. A series of images, like a

scrapbook's unfurling, suddenly took center stage:
Rosa Collins as Nick remembered her, hunched
over old library books and studying Nick's
condition with the zeal of a scholar; Rosa lying
awake at night and contemplating the mystery. It
was ironic – and somewhat sad – that Nick had
taken leave of the one person who could have
potentially helped him.

'I wanted to visit you,' Rosa said, as if reading
his thoughts. 'Many times, I almost did. Only to
back away at the last moment. When your family
left, I knew you would never come back ... not after
what happened to your brother. Though I hoped you
would. You were my opportunity to know more.
What I wanted was to ... *expose* those creatures
somehow. Drag them into the light. They're
cowards, Nick. Creatures who practice a form of
calculated cruelty – like kids pulling the wings off
flies. I said before I don't begrudge you for
introducing me to a world of monsters ... and I
don't. Because *you're* the victim in this. And if
you're back here now to, I don't know, find closure,
then I can only imagine that things never got any
better for you.'

***

Before beginning an account of his own, Nick

took a detour downstairs to relieve his bladder. Then it was onto the kitchen for a plate of finger food and even more wine. Feeling very drunk (despite the sobering conversation), Nick suggested some music might be in order, Alanis Morissette piped through the cabin's Bluetooth speakers from his phone.

'No *Jagged Little Pill*,' Rosa called from upstairs. 'I've had my fill of *that* for a lifetime.'

On the balcony again, Nick watched as an asylum of loons flew over the cabin, their shadows a squadron.

'They did, and they didn't,' Nick said. 'Get better, that is. After I left, there was a period when my episodes stopped altogether. When I was ... free of them.'

There followed an abridged version of events: his second encounter with the underground metropolis, this time chaperoned by Saul. He described stumbling upon something like a lair, one whose doors were painted with the insignia of another world.

'If it wasn't for my brief coma, I wouldn't have remembered any of that. Not in such excruciating detail, anyway.'

Rosa said nothing, but Nick could clearly read her expression: she made the right choice not tempting fate further by returning to the cave.

'Going back ... it tipped me over the edge, somehow. And when I got back to the cabin, Wendy was talking of getting rid of me.'

'Saul let you go?'

'We haven't really spoken of him much, have we? Even now, I hate giving lip service to the man ... to what he might be. And what *is* he, exactly? He's ...'

'The fifth business?' Rosa offered. 'A change agent?'

Nick smiled. 'Or a joker in a deck of cards. The more I think about Saul, the more he mirrors the Devil. Because he was kicked out of somewhere, call it his heaven, and exiled. And it was his job to ... *groom* me for something. Though I haven't the faintest idea for what.'

Rosa said, 'When I was old enough, I looked into island records. It helps if you're a lifelong local.'

'And?'

'And discovered no evidence of any Saul Kidman existing anywhere, in any census. I even scoured old newspapers, convinced his name would turn up somewhere.'

'Nothing?'

'Not so much as a scrap. Did anyone in your family meet him?'

Nick pondered this. 'I'm not sure. Louise might

have mentioned something. If *you* hadn't seen him, I might have convinced myself he never existed at all. That I'd completely imagined him. A kind of surrogate for my real father.'

'Which leads me to my next question,' Rosa said, the first slur infecting her speech. 'Does your family still live in Washington?'

'Louise and Bianca, no. Louise went to Canada to live out her liberal ideals. Bianca lives somewhere in Oregon. We ... almost never speak.'

'I'm sorry.'

'People often think death brings a family closer together. But in my experience, it seems to have the opposite effect.'

'And your parents?'

Nick unconsciously winced, a standard response.

'They're still alive, if that's what you mean. Chad and Wendy live together in a retirement village in Yarrow Point. Wendy is ... Chad's caretaker, I'd guess you'd say. *Still* his caretaker. Chad's third stage Alzheimer's. Cognitive one day, befuddled the next.'

'I'm sorry,' Rosa repeated.

'Don't be.'

'You said ... Wendy's *still* Chad's caretaker?'

'I did, didn't I? That's just the way I've always thought of her. Not his caregiver per say ... more his shadow twin. A modern day Gríma Wormtongue or Piter De Vries.'

This time, Rosa winced. 'You don't speak to him at all anymore?'

'Not since ... probably around the time Clinton was leaving office. When I was almost old enough to drive, Wendy got her wish and pushed me out of the nest. She couldn't do it right away, of course. Not so soon after Sebastian. But when his memory began to dwindle, she made her move.'

'That would have made you ... what? Fifteen? Where did you go?'

'For about two whole years I couch surfed at a friend's house, doing odd things like kitchen work. Later, I started practical photography at Washington University. That's where I met Heidi. We've been together ever since.'

'That must have been hard. Do you blame your father?'

Nick shook his head. 'Not really. We don't speak anymore because Wendy forbids it. Out of all of us, he only talks to Bianca. That's where I get all my information ... from her.'

Lightheaded, Nick pushed back from the balcony and retreated to a plastic chair. Rosa, sensing the mood darken, also took a seat.

She said, 'It's never easy talking about your parents, is it? I don't think I've met a person alive who doesn't have their issues.'

'But *not* talking to my father ... it's never really bothered me. Because the more distance there is between us, the more I like myself. The only vocabulary he knew with me was a kind of passive-aggressive bullying. Almost a weak form of hatred. To him, I was the runt of the litter. That notion wasn't always there, though. It was sort of ... implanted by Wendy. Tough love, he called it. Which I always thought is the moral justification some people give for the pleasure they take in browbeating someone.'

They were close enough that Rosa was able to reach out a hand and place it on his knee. Speaking softly, she said, 'Nick, if his estrangement doesn't bother you, why do you look as if you're going to be sick?'

Seeming to act as a catalyst, the question brought to the surface a deluge of images: Shadow wraiths caught in a camera, their mock hides like oil stains; awakening on Saul's slope the previous evening, a booming hiss of surf below.

Behind his eyelids, Nick felt the subtle prick of tears.

'Isn't it obvious?' he said. 'It's this *place*. Being back in Deception Pass is almost like a form of time travel. And there's stuff I haven't told you about that's happening, that I don't think I *can* tell you –'

'Then *why*?' Rosa asked, her tone more conciliatory than exasperated. 'Why did you come back here? I can't for a minute think your wife and daughter thought it was a good idea for you to come alone. Not at *this* time of the year, anyway.'

Under normal circumstances, Nick's rejoinder would consist of banal reasoning: how the time away from his family was nothing more arbitrary than a chance to recuperate; a spiritual mission. How Heidi acceded to the decision, but there was little use. Rosa would know the lie ... and call him out on it, accordingly.

'I left on a complete whim,' Nick said, the confession like a physical weight removed. 'Told Heidi not to follow me. Of course, she's not happy, and we've hardly spoken. But somehow, I think she knows it's for the greater good. Sebastian's anniversary is approaching. And if I can get through *that*, force myself through it and out the other side, then –'

'You'll be healed somehow?'

'Yes.'

'And by that you mean?'

'Cured of my condition, once and for all. Rosa, it's only gotten worse. And it's only going to *get* worse. Call it avant-garde therapy. My last-ditch effort to ... bury these fucking Shadows for good.'

***

Before going to bed, Nick went through the ritual of securing every door and window, triple checking their locks and peering under tables and beds.

Helen would call this paranoid.

Yes, she undoubtedly would.

But was also likely to endorse it.

Considering everything Nick had endured.

As was habitual, Nick saved his old bedroom for last, convinced on this occasion, it would magically open to his prying fingers. And when it did, a surfeit of revelation would be waiting on the other side.

Not tonight, sweet prince.

Leaning drunkenly against the frame, Nick poked his tongue out and proceeded to run it against the wood. Tonight, despite sharing so much with Rosa, Nick failed to mention this closed and barred room. He also failed to mention the driveway apparitions, his ghost-writing laptop, the photos taken inside the Canlis building, or the specifics of Sebastian's death.

And don't forget your sleepwalking adventures. Last night, you almost became the second Wheeler to take a cliff-dive from Saul's slope.

'Little pigs,' Nick murmured, feeling his cheek

slide down the wood. 'Let me in. Or I'll huff, and I'll puff ...'

Until the Hat Man comes in.

Nick, suddenly fearful, pushed back from the door.

You didn't mention him, either. And why not? Are you so damn superstitious you can't say his name?

'*The Hat Man!*' Nick shouted into the hallway, his voice hoarse. 'The Hat Man, the Hat Man, the fucking Hat Man! Come on out and show yourself! Is that something you can even do anymore while I'm awake? Rosa was right, wasn't she? You're a spineless, lame-ass coward who gets his jollies from frightening little kiddies.' A drunken epiphany bloomed, and Nick quickly seized on it. 'Why, you're no better or worse than a kiddie-fiddler, are you? Just a regular fucking rock spider.'

Hollow entreaties, Nick's words echoed back.

Yet surely Nick's nemesis would finally be revealed. Armed with a scythe, the Hat Man would come barreling down the hallway, primed to mete out his overdue punishment, a merciless end to Nick's prolonged nightmare once and for all.

Instead, Bianca Wheeler staggered into view.

One arm clasping a teddy bear, her piggish eyes held in a rotund face, Bianca turned around to face her brother.

She can't see you. She's just a memory. She can't see you. She's just a memory. She can't –

'Ferris Beel,' Bianca mouthed, and pointed in his direction.

For the first time since stepping into *Deception Tree House*, Nick Wheeler screamed.

<u>7</u>

Nick woke up dead.

Not in a literal sense, he thought.

Familiar panic enveloped him. Attempting to rise from a sleeping position only met resistance; endeavoring to move his head only encountered opposition, like having a vice secured to the side of his skull. Nick's hands, balled into fists, were lead weights pinioned with hooks to the cushions beneath.

Just ... breathe.

The ceiling, his only avenue of sight, afforded Nick something he wasn't prepared for: a chandelier light fixture.

One far removed from the regular bulb above

the Hudson sofa.

I'm in the master bedroom.

Despite going to bed inebriated, Nick clearly recalled crashing on the sofa. This was about half-an-hour, give or take, after his brush with Bianca.

Another act of sleepwalking?

Or somebody moved him.

In the corner of the bedroom – a portion containing an antique rocking chair hidden from sight – Nick detected a presence.

'You were right,' said a voice from the chair.

Intimate with numerous forms of terror, Nick was surprised to feel his dread give way to a new, unplumbed level: the territory of cat and mouse, predator and prey. Another dark, unknown marauder stilled his movements to potentially devour him.

And yet ...

There was something recognizable about its cadence ...

'About the house,' the voice continued. 'What you saw tonight wasn't a ghost. There are no ghosts here. There are only ... memories and moments in time.'

'Saul.'

Surprised he could form a syllable; Nick was equally taken aback he could shift his eyes a fraction – enough to rest them on the hulking form sitting in the rocker.

'Don't bother attempting to see me whole,' Saul replied in his singsong voice. While still mellifluous, its tempo had aged. 'Time in this world has not been kind to me.'

Nick squinted ... and despite Saul's words, he could discern the rudiments of a head, torso, and trench coat. But something was missing, off-kilter. If he could just ...

'Speaking of *time*,' Saul pressed on. 'What conclusions can we draw if we step outside of time and view the human animal from a distance? What terminus do we discover when considering the nature of his evil?'

A man partial to spouting pseudo-metaphysical jargon, Saul seemed to be dusting off his decades' old narrative as if the intervening years never occurred.

'Atrocities *permeate* the human timeline, Nick. We feel their aftereffects throughout history even as they dissipate. This is because they mutate and re-emerge into something else. Evil springs from simple intolerance. And the human species possesses an unwillingness to accept other views differing from their own.'

Becoming increasingly visible, Nick could determine Saul not to have simply aged but succumbed to a species of dissolution. Through the folds of his trench coat, an olive-skinned ribcage protruded.

'You knew, of course, that over two million died during the crusades? And then there's the holocaust. Do they still teach that the Romans burned Christians alive? Coded into the human DNA, there is a quiet malignance. It lives on in the modern era as pathologies of the mind, festering and growing.'

Nick's terror began to ebb, waylaid by the possibility Saul's faculties had also fallen prey to a type of decay. Seeming to sniff Nick's insight, Saul raised a twisted and gnarled hand into the air.

'You can talk to me, Nick,' he said. 'I've bequeathed you some power to do that. Perhaps you would like to know why I'm pontificating on the nature of human evil instead of unleashing the hordes? Or maybe you would like to know why your friend, Rosa, was spared after your vicious stepmother spirited you away from the island?'

'I don't have to,' Nick replied, startled to hear the amount of calm in his voice. 'It was my father's decision to leave here and never return.'

Nick heard a grunt of amusement from the old man's throat, a phlegm-wrapped sound. 'No, it wasn't. Staying away was Wendy's verdict. And do you know why? It had nothing to do with what happened to Sebastian, of course. She cared as much for that whelp as she did for you. No, it was because during that year, Wendy Fuller had her own intimate brush with the Hidden City.'

'More gibberish,' Nick said.

'On the contrary. You know *precisely* what I'm talking about. You and Rosa were discussing it earlier this evening. What did she call it? A *metropolis*. Yes, I believe that was the designation. Quite an apt phrase for the city where the forgotten species of God dwell.'

His arms and legs locked in their perpetual struggle to shift, Nick said, 'I can't decide which is worse – that you associate your realm with God ... or that you spy on me in some fundamental way I'll never understand.'

Saul shifted, the movement displacing a wake of airborne dust. 'You disappoint me, Nick. After everything I taught you, everything I *conveyed* your way, the man I see on that bed is but a willful dullard. There was a time, during the eighth century, when Hellenistic Greeks knew *all* the demonic powers to be divine. Including those arbiter spirits who moved among mortals.'

Despite the cryptic turn, Nick could not hide his outward curiosity. 'Is this a way of saying you're one of these demonic powers? Is the Hat Man?'

'Yes ... and no. Nick, we were talking about

Wendy. About her decision to stay away.'

'Because she knew I was telling the truth?' Nick ventured. 'About the Shadows?'

'Knew it *intimately*, Nick. As do many families who reside in Deception Pass. As did Rosa's father. As did ... your mother.'

This declaration – delivered in Saul's offhand diction – provoked Nick's fear again. His mother? What could *she* have to do with any of this?

'Do you remember, as children, telling Rosa how your mother died? Obstructive sleep apnea? Do you remember telling Rosa that she *died in her sleep*?'

This was something Nick *did* remember. Because they were the same extemporaneous lines his father delivered the morning Kayla passed: *Your mother lived with a disorder. She died peacefully in her sleep.*

Too young to sufficiently grasp the particulars of mortality, Nick thereafter regurgitated the same cavalier lines to all other inquiring minds.

Is Saul trying to tell me my mother suffered the same condition I did?

Tired of waiting for a response, Saul said, 'By nature or nurture, people inherit what belongs to those who came before. And if people are the products of their ancestors, what are the ancestors by-products of? What contrivances are forged at the beginning of their heritage?'

'What does that mean? That what I have is ... hereditary?'

'For some more than others. So many on this island ... are vulnerable to the Hidden City. Your mother was. And you, too. Nick, you are perhaps more vulnerable than any one soul encountered in two hundred years.

'I don't know what that means.'

'Do you recall our talks about quantum mechanics? So much has been discovered since then. Why, your quantum-savvy theorists postulate this universe is but a single reality among billions. And the cosmos itself? One infinite apartment building containing *multiple* universes.'

What came into Nick's mind then wasn't the picture Saul was attempting to paint (worlds bordering each other like rooms), but Deception Pass as it existed in both its past and present state: whole families cut off from the mainland and living together in seclusion. Nick pictured some of these families catching visions in their sleep of another world; they saw the creatures who resided across that world's schism peering back.

Creatures whose substance was immaterial, and whose presence exercised a power to stymie flesh.

'What *is* the Hat Man, you ask? Perhaps he's only a metaphor for a generational curse, a thing *seen* as a man because your species does not possess the sagacity to appropriately measure him. Or perhaps he really *is* one of God's forgotten species, simply a tourist of sorts, navigating the hallways of one infinite apartment building.'

Despite his frozen state – or perhaps because of it –Nick felt anger beginning to supersede his fear, resentment rising like a bubble. Having parceled out a lifetime of ambiguity and deceit, was Saul attempting to provide answers, or simply disperse more suffering?

Nick's sense of being a pawn in this nightmare was aggregate.

'And what about *you*, Saul? Where do *you* fit in? And what the fuck do you want with *me*?'

From the rocking chair came a final and prolonged shuffling.

'What was it you called me earlier? A joker? An exile? That's *just* what I am, Nick. An exile forced to live out his days as a broken thing, cast out of a place I can no longer remember. Do you want to know about the Hidden City? Return there. Go back and discover how time itself provides the architecture.'

<u>8</u>

Showering the next morning, Nick expected his encounter with Saul to disperse, as fleeting as any regular dream.

Because Saul wasn't really there. Whatever condition he subscribes to now is not a material one.

Why, then, could Nick recall every portion of their conversation?

Do you want to know about the Hidden City? Return there. Go back and discover how time itself provides the architecture.

Saul's vocabulary, perpetually mired in metaphor, struck a chord. Earlier, when alluding to ghosts, he reflected the cabin did not contain spirits.

Only ...

'Memories and moments in time,' Nick whispered, stepping out of the shower.

Which reinforced his earlier assumptions concerning Wendy's voice, the smell of her perfume, and even the appearance of Bianca in the hallway.

Moments in time – *past* moments in time – were aligning with the present.

Armed with new insight, Nick's immediate instinct was to pick up the phone and call a certain retirement village in Yarrow Point.

Hi Daddy. How are you? Still senile? That's great. Listen, a lot of shit went down here thirty years ago that you failed to mention. Were you and Wendy seeing ghosts? Did my mother also experience paralysis? Time to fess up, Father – because your only remaining son is also in the process of losing his mind.

For now, Nick resisted the impulse.

First things first.

Shrugging on his best winter jacket and pocketing a camera, Nick Wheeler walked out into a snow-laden day.

***

Thirty years of erosion transformed his path

into a shallow depression that had – in parts –
completely disappeared. With no foot traffic besides
a squirrel and a fox, it was no longer recognizable
as any kind of surefooted map. Guided by intuition,
Nick was able to plot a course back to the cave with
only minor difficulty. And by the time he scaled the
final hill overlooking its weir, the weather cleared,
providing an uninterrupted view of his destination.

Nick's first impression was: *It hasn't changed.*

Then his eyes found the fissure of the tunnel.

In the way of art, an off-beat form of modernity
had taken root. Canvassing the rockface: all manner
of graffiti; a hodgepodge arsenal of aerosol paint.
Art, Nick decided, to provide the impression this
cave was a maw leading directly into Hell.

That word (Hell) was even in evidence.

Spray painted inside a crude arrow.

Like the side of a hot rod, a peacock's plumage
of fire and flame hugged the sediment.

Other designs were suggestive of demonic
entities, the breach their boiling cauldron. While a
few were generic, their tails curled and their
pitchforks three-pronged, many others were
unambiguously ...

Shadow Men.

The same carnival apparitions from Nick's
nightmares given a second life on land.

***

Much like it was when Nick was a boy, descending to the weir was a tricky affair. There were crags to pilot, and portions of the hill smooth enough to ski. Each step, a tightrope-walk to find secure footing, was accompanied by the shriek of seagulls – their din somehow worse than a physical attack.

Minutes later, Nick stood on level ground again, the demonic diorama close enough to touch.

Who did this? Nick kept wondering, and briefly thought of Rosa; the only other person to have dared this darkness.

Rosa never came back.

In the form of a Saul Kidman sentence, a flash of revelation occurred: *So many in Deception Pass ... vulnerable to the Hidden City.*

Nick considered another possibility: conceivably, local adolescents exposed to the mystique of an urban legend. Goaded by nightmares of their own – or by stories of the boy who perished a short distance away.

Several feet from the entrance, Nick pulled out his camera.

In addition to horned beasts, the artists had painted stilted-legged owl-men. One creature, its head a Venus flytrap, brandished candlestick fingers of flickering flame. Others carried the appearance of angels; their bodies beholden with wings in a state of fluttering readiness.

You're not here to sightsee. Not this time.

Nevertheless, Nick took pictures, paying particular attention to the familiar creatures; the proverbial *fiends* who beleaguered his life. Inside the cave proper, Nick's main source of light came from the flash of the camera: an intermittent stroke of lightning that illuminated a menagerie of zoomorphic imps.

Wholly engrossed in the task, Nick failed at first to notice the atmosphere was changing, a shifting of proportions exposing a cavity of earth, once a stream, now devoid of anything but air.

***

The same one we jumped across, Nick thought. *It's completely dry.*

Quartz-like illumination sprouted from rock recesses.

Was the same revolution he'd seen in the drawings (human hands paying homage to something they only perceived) also at work here?

Had the water, smelling the foul workings of another world, simply packed up and left?

Far-fetched as the notion was, evidence for it

waited on the other side: the second tunnel having also fallen prey to entropy; its corners widened and decayed. Suddenly possessed of the same confidence he'd previously harbored, Nick leapt across the divide, the move triggering an immediate effect on an expanse already in the throes of change.

***

In the preceding journey, Nick recalled Rosa's anatomy as they'd entered the second tunnel: her skin (and his) becoming a gross cartoon arrangement, like flesh pulled through a filter.

Once again, a similar process was occurring.

Dark matter as reflective as oil sprouted from his elbows and hands.

Moving with the sentient intent of eels, they first snaked across his chest, and then began to intertwine. The speed of this had the outward show of a practical special effect.

Despite his first instinct to retreat, Nick pressed on.

Though similarities abounded with the past (the darkening environment; the changeling air), another power was laboring here – one whose ambition saw fit to add even more biological matter to Nick's anatomy, liquid tendrils forming the bridgework of a second skeleton.

For a final time, the surrounds altered, soiled earth and rock yielding to a landscape of black glass and churning orange cloud.

The Hidden City.

So much of this veiled world was unchanged ... but there were vast differences, too. Its dwellings – once the size of tenements – were now partial skyscrapers, broad windows reflecting the ginger cloud. Black vegetation (or some derivative of the same) strafed open areas of forest.

Buildings peppered the horizon.

Byzantine streets were busy with life.

They're new and improved, Saul proclaimed in Nick's dream ... a kind of prideful boast concerning the evolution of Shadows.

And here was evidence.

Resembling viruses, lifeforms floated; some of them pockmarked with so many limbs they were like cratered moons. Farther away, toward a range of mountainous hills, Pterodactyl-like birds stood rigid, their bulbous bodies throbbing in the manner of pupates. Below these, smaller genotypes climbed glass structures with the dexterity of worker ants.

For the first time, Nick perceived an order to these beings ... almost a beauty. Because this vista was more in keeping with standard life: survival simply for the sake of it. Existence that brokered no apologies for going about the labor of living.

Perhaps there was something fundamental going on that Nick failed to grasp from the beginning. Again (and with timely precision), it was one of Saul's philosophic phrases which sprung to mind.

Evil springs from simple intolerance. And the human species possesses an unwillingness to accept other views differing from their own.

Was it feasible the Hat Man's realm was *not* some evil dominion?

Speaking around lips that were also succumbing to a dark transformative blight, Nick whispered, 'God's forgotten species navigating the hallways of one infinite apartment building.'

In front of him, the spectacle of Shadows increased, globules of anti-lifelike microorganisms in the throes of replicating.

***

Transported again, Nick felt the sudden constraints of an interior environment. Slowly, he began to apprehend he stood inside a vast room.

Black glass mirrored the reflection of Nick's body.

Grown disproportionately larger, Nick's flesh was a bourgeoning canvas of armor. In lieu of arms, pincer-like appendages had sprouted. Nick's legs, still developing, had flowered into segments like shanks.

Overall, his physique was evocative of a standing centaur.

Beyond the glass, a metropolis, more in keeping with a central nervous system, bustled its citizens glistening with opaque surfaces like spun diamond.

Nick thought: *I'm becoming one of them.*

In a strange way, he was unsurprised. Saul Kidman, unable to penetrate him with words alone, devised a different education.

And here was that schooling.

Temporary access to the anatomy of Shadows.

While this metamorphosis fell short of the hierarchy outside, there was enough evolution here to suggest Nick fit the profile of an earlier model; his exterior not dissimilar to those fledging creatures who scuttled from the culverts to intercept two children a lifetime ago.

As Nick watched, more organic matter – the fused bones of a plastron carapace – bloomed through his upper body.

Unable to slow the spread, only observe it, Nick saw his head also succumb to a dark mutation.

A final ingredient to seeing this world anew.

Seeing *two* worlds anew.

Earth.

Lapping at the periphery of this Hidden City, a world of ocean, land ... and invertebrate completely at odds with their environment.

A short time ago, Nick likened his tormentors to a virus.

From what he saw now, the *opposite* was true.

Human beings are the scourge.

A species that saw fit to attack its living host in order to replicate; a cyclic disease that could never be quieted or killed.

The human world was spilling into this one.

Perhaps the most astonishing revelation of all.

The Shadow species perceived its adjacent civilization to be an interloper; a trespassing peril.

Your tribe, came a voice from Nick's right*, possesses an unwillingness to accept other views differing from their own.*

Though he didn't need to turn around to recognize the owner of the voice, Nick did so anyway. His new vision, through a shifting spectrum of sound, afforded him the ability to observe the Hat Man in a fundamentally different light.

Garbed in a Top Hat for the occasion, Nick gazed upon a changed physiognomy; the mimicry of a hundred different species struggling to be born. One minute, the flicker of an antelope's eyes. The next, a spider's even-pronged tier.

You see now, don't you? the Hat Man said. *You see the stain in your species?*

And God help him, Nick did. Humanity, repressed and inhibited by its own limited senses, had an established history in the subjugation of other life forms it did not understand.

And what it failed to understand, it vilified.

There has never been any reason to fear me, Nick.

In spite of his state, Nick could have laughed. *Why* then? Why the endless hours of midnight terror? Why this secrecy? Why the monstrous manifestations and malevolent threats? What purpose had it served to cause him pain while delivering umbrous ultimatums?

What *rationale* existed for murdering his brother on an icy slope?

Sensing his confusion, the Hat Man spoke again. Not with words this time, but a series of images every bit as nuanced as his view of the Hidden City.

Having discovered doorways into the human kingdom, the Shadow species began entering the homes of a thousand different lives over a thousand different generations. At first, they were only curious explorers of a new frontier ... then, taken aback by what they perceived as a negative menace.

Nick beheld this first contact – witnessed

Shadow Men stepping through rents in time where the walls were thin. And saw human paralysis becoming an inadvertent side-effect of greeting a force that existed outside the sphere of time.

Time.

An epiphany as elusive as it was obvious; a final mystery solved.

The Hat Man (and his circus of freaks) were time travelers.

9

When Nick finally arrived back at the cabin, it was past midnight; his last leg of the return journey a blur of sleet and cold. While he remembered little of leaving the cave, the events inside were sharp enough to cast his living quarters in an intimidating new light.

Despite the forbidding occurrences inside, the house was supposed to serve as a healing retreat: a doorway to reconciling the past.

Yet seeing it surface from the snow, its steeple ominously phallic, promptly filled Nick with a sense of foreboding so acute he almost stumbled and fell before reaching the steps.

There is no help coming.

You're all alone.

With no Heidi to dispense solace, and no Hayley to provide care, Nick felt as helpless as an infant left in the woods to die: a naked lifeform at the mercy of wolves.

Get inside. Call Rosa if you have to. Just don't succumb to despair. Not now – not with the endgame so close.

Minutes passed. With a gentle snow falling, Nick finally found the impetus to move, mounting each step with the crestfallen amble of someone defeated.

***

This time, there was no sensation of waking or swimming up from a tide of dreams. One instant, Nick had been in the throes of non-existence. The next, a delirium of paralysis so concentrated his previous episodes felt like warmups.

Concrete engirdled his body.

I can't even feel my heart.

'Your heart continues to beat,' came Saul's voice from the corner. 'And you can talk – should you feel the desire. Or would you prefer to just listen?'

'Why?' Nick asked, the effort like trying to form words around food. 'When you can just read my mind?'

'Not true,' said Saul. 'Perhaps only *partially* true. I can hear snippets, like your voice coming from an adjacent room – but nothing overly dramatic. Nick, we're connected. Or haven't you worked that out yet?'

I've worked that out. I've just never understood the why.

A standard shifting sound came from Saul adjusting his bulk. Though presently undiscernible as a whole, he sensed the old man smiling.

Nick's thought (that time) had come through loud and clear.

'The why? I think it might be time for me to *tell* you the why. After all, our endgame *is* near. But first ... have you had time to reflect on what you were shown tonight? The dark miracle of it? It's not often someone gets to wear our skin and see through our eyes.'

'*Your* skin? What *you* see?'

His teacher demeanor returned; Saul was nodding. 'Yes, my skin. They were a tribe I belonged to once – but you know that already, don't you? Nick, I *existed* in that eternity.'

'Were you thrown out?'

His tone uncomfortable, Saul replied, 'No. I was ... given a mission. What humans might think of as reconnaissance. I was to examine the lay of the land, wearing one of *your* skins. Back then, I was a nameless creature wandering the blind face of a distant land.'

'Nameless?'

'I was born a man and anointed by no one. So, I decided to anoint myself. Saul is the name of the first king of Israel, whose mission was to unite their tribes. And Kidman … the original metonymic simply means goat-herder – or a man in charge of kids.'

If Nick possessed the capacity to laugh, he would have done so. Because his previous suspicion of the Hat Man being a kind of pervert now had an undeniable air of truth.

'Were there other children, then? Besides me?'

'*Of course,* there were other children. I knew children of the Upper Skagits and the Lower Skagits. I witnessed British Colombian tribes raid their island and take slaves. I saw smallpox, for which there was no immunity, claim lives by the hundreds.'

Christ, Nick thought. *He's talking about Native Americans.*

'Why?'

'Why what?'

'Why *children*? Why were you sent here?'

'Because *he* demanded it,' Saul answered.

There was no need to push further. Because in

this equation, there had only ever been one *he*.

A creature who, for some unfathomable purpose, collected different hats like a jack of all trades.

'And what does *he* want with children?'

'Your company.'

As a justification, it felt both outlandish and implausible.

A time-traveling entity plucking out human children like sushi on a conveyor belt.

'He only wants to understand you, Nick. Understand your species. So, I was tasked with finding a familiar for him. A ... proxy.'

'But you failed in that endeavor, didn't you? Just like the first king of Israel.'

'I *haven't* failed. Because he's giving you a second chance. Even as a grown man, he's giving you another opportunity to sit beside him. And, having seen through his eyes, traveled to his City –'

'The Devil *lies*,' Nick spat. 'Painting *us* as the villains in his story! A menace. No matter how many dark miracles you show me, I won't believe that.'

Pain – as sudden and sharp as a splash of boiling water – coiled through Nick's intestines.

Three-pronged and livid, the scythe had returned.

'Do you think this is some kind of game?'

came the voice from the rocking chair. 'You were *chosen*. Why would you continue to deny him?'

With the pain beginning to subside, Nick said, 'That isn't obvious? Even now, you continue to hurt me. Not long ago, you almost killed me. Did you forget that my brother was murdered? He was torn apart while I watched, for Christ sake, then carried off like an offering.'

Seeming to weigh something that vexed him, Saul said, 'I don't pretend to understand my boss's motivations all the time, Nick. He can be ... capricious. It is my understanding he wanted you as a willing participant. The ultimatum was an experiment. And you weren't the first to undergo it. With other subjects, similar bargains have been struck.'

'What really happened to him? What happened to Sebastian? In my dream, I saw him as something else.'

Saul guffawed. '*That* was just a parlor trick on my part, I'm afraid. One designed to summon you here. But an impressive parlor trick, wouldn't you say?'

'My brother –'

'Is both nowhere and everywhere. The last time you saw him, he was on our slope. Nick, he's *still* there. As are we, watching the sky together through my binoculars. We've always *been* there. Because

263

time is only a *human* construct. This you have recently learned. But it's a construct we can ultimately separate from, if you know how.'

For the briefest moment, Nick was able to force his eyes downward ... and what he saw in the corner confounded him.

Saul Kidman as part man; part smoke. His gaunt frame leaning forward with a kind of rueful expectancy.

'What do I mean by that? In a few nights, you'll know. You see, a graph must be formed. And it will open the door to your past. Once again, you will have to make a choice. A *final* choice. Join us or choose to live here forever as a prisoner of time.'

Flooding back: Nick's time in the Hidden City; his metamorphosis into Shadow and sprouting a new anatomy.

One that wasn't subject to dissolution or time.

'You talk of parlor tricks,' Nick said, hoping to change the subject. 'What were those creatures in my driveway? The messages on my computer? Were they also parlor tricks?'

Saul's response was swift.

'The walls are getting thinner, Nick. Just like they were before. Knowing what's about to transpire, tourists from the Hidden City are crossing the divide.'

'And what about my family? Their voices –'

'*Time* is getting thinner. Its architecture is fraying.'

Hoping its vehemence was enough to reach the entity across the room, Nick thought: *And I'm your ticket home, aren't I? You finally secure the proxy, and your boss decides to open the gates of the Hidden City for good?*

No answer from the rocking chair.

Instead, Saul unleashed another torrent of pain, his invisible scythe like a serrated blade.

10

In the afternoons, with Greg Golden's storm surge a real possibility, Nick took walks on remote trails he'd seldom seen, let alone visited. With no camera to document things for posterity, only his eyes, Nick bore witness to the secret life of Deception Pass.

Boasting cliff-edge views, grassy headlands gave way to booming sea and far off mountains. Bereft anything besides quarrelling bufflehead – a duck so gossamer it was ornamental – the beaches were a picturesque postcard of clean sand and piles of driftwood.

Despite the beauty, Nick felt the ominous presage of time.

And the presence of another world.

Sometimes, it was just a suggestion, a flitting of shade like a passing fox. Other times (when staring at Goose Rock, for instance), Nick caught sight of gargoyle-like creatures quietly observing him from behind the camouflage of trees.

Tourists from the Hidden City, crossing the divide.

At night, with the December wind shrieking through the eaves, *Deception Tree House* again came alive, the sounds of the past travelling through the kitchen and hallway like the phantom echo of a TV sitcom. Once, Nick distinctly heard Louise Wheeler sobbing into a pillow. Later, he discovered the ephemeral form of his stepmother hunched over a porcelain sink in the bathroom.

If she sensed Nick's presence, she failed to show it.

Staring into the mirror, Wendy consulted her reflection with the agitated look of a bully who only knew pain.

***

The fourteenth of December finally arrived.

After a belated supper, Nick was drying his dishes and thinking about wine when a gentle knock carried into the kitchen from the backdoor.

His first impression – that he heard the thud of a snowball – was waylaid by the repeated knocking.

Insistent.

And gentle.

Having endured weeks of isolation, Nick felt an old and familiar anxiety spiraling up through his ribcage like an invading spirit.

Only Rosa knows you're here.

If it's her – why is she knocking on the backdoor?

Since their parting last Saturday night, only a few customary texts were exchanged: Rosa wanting to know how he was fairing; wanting to know if he was eating all right. Nick replied in the affirmative, politely declining her offer of company when she'd floated the idea of bringing him something homemade.

Hoping the enforced silence would be enough to send any intruder packing, Nick held his breath and remained stationary.

More urgent, the knocking came again.

Sidling through the hallway, Nick began thumbing off light switches. Reaching the laundry, he paused before entering its spill of light, knowing his presence would be revealed.

Leaving the lights on is a child's habit, he remembered Heidi once admonishing him. *Are you a child, Nick?*

No, he wasn't. But he had been. In this very cabin, no less. Could he be blamed for falling back into old habits?

Wind pressed against the backdoor, demanding entry.

From the other side, another series of knocks issued.

Stepping into the laundry, Nick tiptoed to the window and froze. Catching sight of his own reflection.

It was the light, of course – shielding him from seeing *through* the window. Shielding him from –

'Nick?'

The voice outside was meek, distinctly female.

'Are you there, Nick? Please open up.'

Not Rosa.

But a voice as familiar as his own heartbeat.

Through the window, Heidi Wheeler's profile abruptly bled into being, the bob of her auburn hair positioned above a faux-fur collar.

Seeing him, her face brightened into a smile.

His fear forgotten and his relief total, Nick busied himself opening the door, so he could usher his wife inside.

***

At first, there was only room for gratitude and

kisses.

Though Nick felt pressed to assail Heidi with questions *(What are you doing here? How did you get here?)*, he decided instead to accept the moment.

Heidi had come for him.

This was all that mattered.

Coursing his fingers through his wife's hair, Nick began to lament his decision of ever coming to Deception Pass. For some unfathomable reason, he'd chosen a cold and desolate cabin over the woman he loved.

Never again.

Never would Nick put his selfish desires above the needs of his family.

Soon, they would return home.

Together.

And damn everything and everyone else.

Including the demons who summoned him here.

Accepting of Nick's kisses, Heidi began to demand more. After removing his top, she raked her fingers down his chest. Then lowered them past his midsection and started stroking.

As abruptly as they'd begun, Nick ceased his affections and pulled back from Heidi's lips and eyes.

Her eyes were distant.

Faraway.

Stabbing through his awareness, a clear and troubling thought.

Where's Hayley?

Slowly, he eased away even further; the damning logic of his daughter's whereabouts taking center stage. If Heidi crossed from the mainland alone ...

Then Hayley was alone.

Nick comprehended how strangely improbable this reunion was. Heidi, wordless since entering, braved insurmountable odds to arrive here. Overcome with surprise and longing, Nick hadn't thought twice before letting her in.

Letting what in?

'Heidi?' Nick asked, taking a full step back and almost tripping in the process. Heidi's skin – a charged white – had the pristine hue of alabaster.

'Heidi?' Nick asked again, but his words were impinged by his cheeks abruptly stuffed with cotton; his mouth full of marbles.

In past instances when the miraculous had taken hold, it was often Saul's voice Nick heard; Saul offering up his damnable and inane logic.

This time, Nick heard the voice of the Hat Man.

Look at that creature.

A thing completely at odds with its environment.

On the precipice of change, Nick's body tensed.

He'd felt its type recently, of course – inhabiting the strange laws of that other world, his reflection in the throes of an evolutionary upheaval.

Nick felt, then *saw*, the same changes being wrought.

Thrusting outward, his back bulged with plates of armor. Glistening material – black, coiled, and grossly membranous – grew from his fingers and replaced them with claws.

Also succumbing to the body's revolution, Nick's eyes regarded the thing standing in his living room with new insight.

A thing wired to be bad.

Bad, blinkered, and vain.

Human beings were a dogmatic, narrow-minded animal that subjugated other lifeforms.

Hardly even deserving of life.

In one fluid motion, Nick crossed the room; his new anatomy affording him the ability to strike cobra-like.

With lithe lethality, his claws sliced through Heidi's neck: first her jugular, then windpipe, the sheer force of bloodletting bringing the human to her knees. Emboldened by the amputation, additional pincers sprouted along Nick's elbow, a scabbard of them.

Tearing into Heidi's stomach, the blunt trauma unleashed a spill of rank and steaming innards. Teetering forward, she slumped into a widening pool of blood.

***

Sudden movement caught Nick's attention.

A reflection in the plain mirror mounted above the fireplace.

His own.

Through this mirror, Nick beheld a human being squatting on all fours.

No carapace adorned this human.

Nor claws.

Reflected at its feet, the butchered prey was not Heidi Wheeler; *not* the woman who had entered through the backdoor moments ago.

This woman was shorter with dazzling red hair and shamrock eyes.

Not possible.

The dead woman was Rosa Collins.

***

Another parlor trick?

More fuel for Saul's fire?

Used like a marionette, Nick had been

deceived.

Loathe to return his eyes to the real world again, Nick grudgingly did so, hoping the mirror's reflection had been as illusory as his transformation.

Arms splayed like alms; Rosa Collins lay dead.
I killed her.

His hands fully returned to a human state; Nick inspected the murder weapons, felt a species of self-loathing hitherto endured.

From the hallway came a sound, unheard since his arrival, its prolonged din somehow musical.

His bedroom door finally opening.

***

Light emanated from his old bedroom, a crimson torrent that bathed every inch of *Deception Tree House*.

Nick stood up.

With measured steps, he edged toward the bedroom.

My ultimate destiny was inside the cabin all along. Just waiting for the right time to open.

But what did his ultimate destiny comprise?

Was this another doorway into the Hidden City? Perhaps the anteroom to an altogether *different* world ...

It's neither of those things.

No, it wasn't. And as Nick walked the final steps, he could *feel* why.

The Hidden City, a fractured place outside of time, was still only a place. But lurking inside this cavalcade light was something infinitely grander: the scaffolding of time itself.

Perceiving his presence, the crimson light erupted into forms, groping vines like sentient tree roots.

Inviting Nick to travel to a world beyond ghosts, beyond moments in time.

11

Night wind.

Booming surf and sea.

Crimson light gave way to a rocky cliff-face beneath a firmament of stars.

Saul's slope.

Nick's journey through the bedroom schism altered his flesh yet again. From his back, wings sprouted. From his shoulder blades, grapplers like an animal's ungula.

Close by were brethren Shadows, raised from idleness by Nick's sudden appearance.

They were waiting for me ...

No, not for him.

Waiting for the humans coming up the slope.

Two young boys in the snow.

It was December 1984.

When Nick would make a choice …

To join them.

Or choose to live in the world forever as a prisoner of time.

Aided by preternatural senses, Nick heard the first intimations of human sound: boys' voices raised in bickering.

What is he, anyway? one boy was saying. *A hobo? A bum? What the hell is he doing outside at this time of the night?*

He lives underground, in the caves, came the reply. *At least some of the time. During the day, he never leaves his slope. Tonight, will be different, though. He'll be waiting for me.*

The words, perhaps acting as a summons, ushered into being a presence on Nick's left.

A final piece of symmetry.

In the form of Saul.

Brandishing his cane, Nick's old mentor beamed.

Seeing him, Nick comprehended the ultimatum – what was being asked of him. Saul's boss, the Hat Man, wanted to secure his proxy with a show of loyalty.

And be his brother's executioner.

As he surely had been from the start.

With the thought, a memory resurfaced: scaling this slope, Nick glimpsed, all too briefly, *his* face in the throng of waiting demons.

Internally, Nick could hear the voice of the Hat Man, a sibilant whisper, demanding that Nick make his choice *now*.

The Hat Man.

Even now, Nick had trouble understanding his would-be antagonist and liberator. A generational curse, Saul had boasted.

A forgotten species.

But what is he really?

Another deceiver, Nick thought.

A god promising eternity, but instead showing terror, death, and illusions.

Finally taking to the air on tenebrous wings, it wasn't the Hat Man that occupied Nick's thoughts ... it was Rosa. An innocent who paid the ultimate price for Nick's weakness.

Someone who, by their actions, unwittingly championed Nick's final decision.

Below, sprinting in fear, Sebastian toppled over, screaming into the snow as his executioners approached.

Though it wasn't Sebastian Nick flew toward.

It was young Nicholas Wheeler, his satisfied features grown suddenly afraid.

Seeing the Shadows had come for him at last.

Epilogue

All morning, Mitchell complained about the weather (when wasn't *he complaining?). Rosa decided she'd rather be outside suffering the weather than spend another minute under the same roof as a belligerent brother who made wintering in Deception Pass more unbearable than regular life back home.*

His whining was bad – even worse was their mother's stubborn refusal to put a stop to it.

Her hangovers – out in force recently – often watered down any natural ability she possessed to appropriately discipline her son.

At least I can go *outside, Rosa thought, shrugging into her mittens and boots. Stepping out onto the porch, she inhaled a morning fresh with snow.*

Poor Nick Wheeler wasn't so lucky.

Not after the stunt they pulled together.

Grounded, he'd told her over the phone. Probably for a while, too. So, there was a good chance Rosa wouldn't be seeing him again anytime soon – perhaps for the rest of the winter.

And it was all her fault.

No, she corrected herself.

It wasn't *her fault. How could Rosa have possibly predicted they would walk into a nightmare world populated by strange monsters?*

Walking past her mailbox, Rosa shivered. Now, days later, she still struggled to comprehend what really happened.

Or if those events happened at all.

There was no sense in fooling herself.

Nick's monsters were real.

And maybe, with a bit of sleuthing, Rosa could eventually discover how *real...*

***

Branches stirred in the wind. Far away came the sound of a small plane, its lazy drone mosquito-like. Pausing, Rosa took a moment to revel in the surrounds, her appreciation of them fueled by knowing these roads and cabins would – very soon – be filled with hundreds of summer tourists. And then the mystique would vanish as –

Through the trees, other sounds intruded.

Raised voices.

The chitter-chatter of people.

Rosa's walking route, initially random, had seen her emerge into a clearing of Douglas firs. Parked nearby, a small array of cars stood sentry.

Her first thought – that she had stumbled onto a camping site – was apprehended after noticing one of the cars was a Fire and Rescue Jeep. Strobing in lazy arcs, its bubble-top colored the surrounding foliage green and red.

Rosa's second thought: Something's happened to Nick.

That idea was given weight the closer she came, edging toward a small throng of people who had, thus far, failed to notice her.

The group stood in a rough semi-circle on a dirt path.

The same path Rosa had intercepted Nick on days ago.

One from the group wore a ranger's uniform, seemingly standing guard.

Blocking the way forward.

Before they could see her, Rosa ducked behind a tree. Gingerly, she made her way through a maze of small boulders until she stood level with the path. Something – call it instinct – urged her to be cautious. To not give away her presence or position.

Otherwise, she too would be blocked.

Without consideration, using the same courage she fronted when jumping the underground stream with Nick, Rosa began powerwalking. Soon, her momentum became enough for her to slip past the uniformed guard.

***

The scene was chaotic, reminiscent of a movie.

More rangers crowded the slope, perhaps five in all. Talking and waving, they gestured people back from the edge. Bystanders, some still covered in sleeping robes, some inhaling cigarettes, stared out at the sea with awkward horror.

Two adults she recognized as Nick Wheeler's parents.

Three kids, his siblings.

Tiptoeing, Rosa came closer, her core attention reserved solely for Nick's brother.

Sebastian, she remembered.

Having drifted away from his family, Sebastian snatched troubled looks at the sky and slope as if trying to piece together the ultimate mystery of life.

Then his eyes found hers.

He looked, Rosa thought, like someone completely unsurprised to see her standing there.

Feeling unreal, feeling like she was in a dream, Rosa broached the remaining distance until they stood only inches apart. Like his family, Sebastian still wore his pajamas, his hair covered with a bright yellow beanie.

Dark smudges underlined eyes stained with tears.

Though knowing what the answer would be, Rosa asked, 'What happened?'

Wiping his nose, Sebastian replied, 'Nick fell. Last night. I was there. I saw it.'

Rosa could only hold to silence.

'They're having trouble getting him back up. It's dangerous. So, they're sending a boat. Before, Dad tried to go down by himself. You know, to see, but the rangers wouldn't let him.'

Rosa moved her gaze back toward the mourning couple: Chad and Wendy – both draped in blankets.

'He's dead?' Rosa asked.

'Yes. You knew him a little, didn't you?'

'I ... yes,' Rosa replied, unsure of how to proceed. 'We knew each other.'

Sebastian said, 'They're going to say it was an accident.'

'Was it?'

Nick's brother regarded her sheepishly. 'Not in the way they think.'

He knows, Rosa thought.

He knows about the Shadows.

'I should go back home,' Rosa said. 'Perhaps you can tell me about it later?'

His gaze returned to the slope; Sebastian nodded.

Longing to take one final look at Nick's family, Rosa's eyes instead alighted on the sea. Hidden until now, sunlight had broken through the cloud cover, spangling the strait of Deception Pass in a corona of intense white.

Though Nick's body lay somewhere down below, it wasn't hard for Rosa to imagine he shared space with all that blinding light.

Such a place, Rosa thought, would have little room for shadows.

October 2018 – February 2020
Adelaide, Australia

ABOUT THE AUTHOR

A vociferous horror columnist since 2005, Matthew Tait published his first collection of dark fiction in 2011. Since then, he has twice been nominated for the Australian Shadows Award. Described as writing 'the sort of horror Clive Barker must read on his days off,' Matthew's fiction often treads the line between the familiar and the fantastic.